Aagol

Kabilan Vairamuthu is a multi-faceted Tamil writer known for his work as a novelist, screenwriter, poet, and lyricist. Kabilan published his first book at the age of 18.

He has donned many hats in the Tamil film industry too. He has penned screenplays, dialogues, and lyrics to numerous films. His poetry collections include *Ulagam Yaavaiyum*, *Endraan Kavingan*, *Manithanukku Aduthavan*, *Kadavulodu Pechuvaarthai*, and *Mazhaiku Othungum Manbommai*. His novels *Boomerang Bhoomi*, *Uyirchol*, *Meinigari*, *Aagol*, and his short story collection *Ambarathooni* are intriguing efforts delving with the past, present, and future.

Kabilan pursued his masters in Communication for Social Change at the University of Queensland, Australia. Kabilan Vairamuthu's diverse talents have made him a prominent figure in contemporary Tamil literature.

Meera Ravishankar is a lawyer, an educationist, a language and communication trainer, and a writer and translator. She loves taking on challenges and is happy to straddle many worlds, whether writing textbooks for school children, training corporate, developing content, or translating. Meera has done bilingual translations in Tamil and English. Her notable translations into Tamil are by Chetan Bhagat, Amish Tripathi, Anand Neelakantan, Rujuta Diwekar, and Kevin Missal. Her English translation of Sujata's *Anita: A Trophy Wife* has been published by Rupa Publications.

Meera bagged the Tamil Nadu State Award for the Best Translator, 2021.

Meera's translation of *Modi@20: Dreams Meet Delivery* was released by the Governor of Puducherry and at the Kasi Tamil Sangamam by the Home Minister Amit Shah.

Aagol

Kabilan Vairamuthu

Translated by
Meera Ravishankar

RUPA

Published by
Rupa Publications India Pvt. Ltd 2024
7/16, Ansari Road, Daryaganj
New Delhi 110002

Sales centres:
Bengaluru Chennai Hyderabad
Jaipur Kathmandu Kolkata
Mumbai Prayagraj

Copyright © Kabilan Vairamuthu 2024
Translation copyright © Mysticswrite Private Limited 2024

This is a work of fiction. Names, characters, places and incidents
are either the product of the author's imagination or are used
fictitiously and any resemblance to any actual person, living
or dead, events or locales is entirely coincidental.

All rights reserved.

No part of this publication may be reproduced, transmitted
or stored in a retrieval system, in any form or by any means,
electronic, mechanical, photocopying, recording or otherwise,
without the prior permission of the publisher.

P-ISBN: 978-93-5702-831-8
E-ISBN: 978-93-5702-747-2

First published in Tamil in 2022

First published in English by Rupa Publications India Pvt. Ltd.
in association with Mysticswrite Private Limited

First impression 2024

10 9 8 7 6 5 4 3 2 1

The moral right of the author has been asserted.

Printed in India

This book is sold subject to the condition that it shall not,
by way of trade or otherwise, be lent, resold, hired out or otherwise
circulated, without the publisher's prior consent, in any form of
binding or cover other than that in which it is published.

Contents

Name and Address… 9
Translator's Note 11

000000000001 15
000000000002 20
000000000003 24
000000000004 27
000000000005 31
000000000006 34
000000000007 38
000000000008 42
000000000009 45
000000000010 48
000000000011 51
000000000012 56
000000000013 59
000000000014 61
000000000015 67
000000000016 72
000000000017 75
000000000018 77
000000000019 84
000000000020 89
000000000021 92
000000000022 94

000000000023	99
000000000024	102
000000000025	104
000000000026	109
000000000027	115
000000000028	120
000000000029	126
000000000030	128
000000000031	133
000000000032	140
000000000033	145
000000000034	150
000000000035	155
000000000036	157
000000000037	165
000000000038	170
000000000039	176
000000000040	184
000000000041	186

To the brave souls who sacrificed their lives at the Perungamanallur riots…

Name and Address...

'*Aagol*' in Tamil would mean 'capturing the cattle.' There is evidence in the inscriptions about the conquering kings taking over the cattle of the vanquished kings and their lands. In the Sangam era, when battles broke out between feudatory kings, they would capture the enemy's goats and cows. Capturing the cattle is the first act in a war. It was looked at as a brave deed, but on the flip side, it was also condemned as theft.

As times change, words lose their context. To save the meaning of a word and hold on to its original sense I feel that the depth of the word and its meaning must be deepened. Cows and goats were the enemy's wealth. It may be considered that, if one captures the enemy's wealth, he loses his strength. It may be further considered that looting the enemy's wealth weakens him. I have titled my fourth novel on this basis. I take great pride in inviting a second-century word to the twenty-first century! Welcome—Aagol!

The modern world is expanding at a fast pace. It is expanding in all directions and we are unable to grasp its growth! Many among us do not have the heart to accept that we cannot comprehend its growth and expansion. We follow its diktat and its course and hence we live in an illusion of cheer that we are updating ourselves on the go. It is a satisfaction of sorts.

Writers do not live long in mere satisfaction. My story's effort is to gaze at the future through the windows of the past.

Aagol is a fictitious tale spun around some unforgettable incidents. It overspills its natural boundaries and makes a quantum leap in fantasy fiction based largely on imagination. The characters are sensitive and special and cannot reveal themselves, so it is recommended that you follow them keenly and carefully.

This journey contains two different exemplary experiences and my heartfelt gratitude to the technicians, research scholars, and writers who stood by me.

Thanks to Rupa Publications for bringing *Aagol* to the English scene.

I invite you to the world of *Aagol* with great love and ofcourse a sound warning!

Kabilan Vairamuthu

Translator's Note

The translator is the author's accomplice, and I am privileged to be a part of this journey called Aagol, with Kabilan Vairamuthu. I went into the vortex of this time capsule many-a-time to ensure that my translation transforms everything into English but nothing really changes of the original!

The warp and weft of the fabric of Kabilan's *Aagol* are technology, history, and anthropology on the one hand, and individuals collectively struggling to retain their identity on the other.

Could it possibly be: a science fiction that includes time travel and the threat of a digital apocalypse? A geopolitical fantasy fiction on digital wars? Is it a historical account of the heart-rending story of the villagers of Perungamanallur who fought for their rights against the Criminal Tribes Act in British India? I would say all of these and much more.

Twenty-first century dawns with its set of bouquets and brickbats. Technological evolution is at its zenith. Science has given humans the leverage of information which is the key to power.

Every possible aspect of life is data, and the overarching concept is that larger, more intricate datasets, particularly those derived from emerging data sources with increasing volumes, constitute the formidable realm of big data. Human beings succumb to power and sometimes forget that with great power comes great responsibility. Data is the pass key to intrude, invade, and take over a person's details and identity.

Every century sees its share of war. The strategies and tools essentially differ. The spirit of conquest, the spoils of war, and the abuse of power—these don't seem to change.

The digital era sees digital wars and digital attacks. These cyber attacks are usually aimed at accessing, changing, or destroying sensitive information. The world has lived many apocalypses—floods, deluge, natural disasters, meteoric attacks and is now on the verge of a digital apocalypse.

Cyber security is the only resort to protect systems, networks, and programs from digital attacks; but it is not impenetrable!

The book discusses all of this as a current or rather futuristic backdrop, and then there is a deeper undercurrent of British India's power struggle! The Criminal Tribes Act was brought in by the Britishers to criminalise entire Indian communities by categorising them as habitual criminals. Because of this label, restriction on their movements was also imposed. They were designated criminals and put under continuous surveillance.

Flash backward to the third century BC, Sangam era, where Aagol was a practice amongst the kings—cattle and goats were grabbed as war spoils and the sustenance of the vanquished would be put under threat.

The crux of the matter is to restrain people with what they hold precious across the centuries: cows and goats, fingerprints, or biometrics.

Flash forward to 2032, and the protagonist Nithilan, a vulnerability analyst, is a troubleshooter who creates programs and algorithms to 'set things right,' and as the plot thickens, he establishes that, 'To fight and conquer in all your battles is not supreme excellence; supreme excellence consists in breaking the enemy's resistance without fighting.'*

Men break worlds, men make worlds and the world goes on!

I would recommend you to fasten your seat belts as you tumble into this time capsule: In the words of Charles F.

---

*Sun, Tzu, *The Art of War*, Hachette, UK, 1994.

Glassman, 'expect the unexpected; experience the familiar that is unfamiliar, make the unknown known, believe the unbelievable, and, of course get a little uncomfortable!'

Meera Ravishankar

Madurai—South outer street—Vandipettai's Sami verandah. Aanachathan's whole team was slumbering around like bats that had slipped down on the ground. They were feigning sleep. They were checking the readiness and functionality of their various weapons—spears, slingshots, small pebbles, sickles, sharp knives, small crowbars, and country ropes that they carried.

'Hey! Do not lick on the marijuana balls Valiya! They are for the dogs!' Aana warned Valiyan who had them rolled up in his dhoti.

Aanachathan was quite aware that Valiyan could not contain his hunger. Aana had done some safekeeping of marinated and dried short eats and onion balls rolled up in his dhoti in case they needed first aid during the theft attempt. He had mentally planned and willed them for Valiyan to eat, after the theft.

'Aana, the iguana is getting restless. It wants to come out,' commented Valiyan, for he was carrying an iguana for a theft for the first time.

'Hey Chinnasami, give that stone to the iguana for it to bite and take it away quickly. Give it a shot!'

As per Aana's instruction, he picked one of the pebbles that he had reserved for the slingshot from his bundle. He opened a fraction of the lid of the coir box that carried the iguana, showed the pebble and quickly withdrew his hand. Maybe because it had bitten into something that it should not, or because it had the satisfaction of clenching its jaw around something solid, whatever it was, on the high of having made a successful attempt, the iguana stayed quiet and motionless for some time.

The team stood up and stretched their arms and started moving towards the path that Aanachathan pointed. They moved like black worms crawling on the undulated land carefully, in single file, and entered the Agraharam. The roads which had witnessed the run of bullock carts and horse carts during the day, were engulfed by the darkness of the night.

The third floor of the second house in Colonel Heron Street was one of the houses, which functioned as an office where income tax officers and revenue officials post their raids, had stocked the confiscated goods of the people who had evaded taxes. Rice sacks, mud pots, blunt plows, dhotis, earrings, cauldrons, hens, white goats—there were things and livestock, and the rooms that stocked these on the third floor smelt of treasure. But then Aanachathan had no intent of stealing any of these.

A khaki-clad watchman was fast asleep with his head resting on his hat.

'We used to be half-asleep like watchdogs and stay alert! But look at this buffalo, who has pledged the city to them! I wonder if we faulted Lord Shiva in any way!'

Aanachathan, who was known for his majesty, now felt belittled and hung his head in shame when he spoke these painful words and his whole team was shaken by his pain and stood still in bewilderment. It would be dawn in a few hours and they had to swing into action, so the Kalappanpatti youth sped into their activities.

Aanachathan opened the coir box, lifted the iguana by firmly holding its tail and legs and shoved a piece of meat that he had carried for this purpose into its mouth. Then he tied the sturdy country rope around its back and threw the iguana towards the third floor.

It held on to a grill on the window. The country rope was hanging down from the iguana, and taking a good grip on it, Valiyan and Chinnasami quickly climbed up. Valiyan realised that time was running out and that he could not trust the grip of the iguana anymore. So, he untied the rope from its body and tried to tie it around himself. While he was untying the knot, it slipped from his fingers and the rope slid down.

'Hey, idiot! Should I come flying up? I should whack my head with a stout guava stick for having inducted you into the team!'

One wondered if Aanachathan truly became angry, as his temper flares seemed to flash and then douse on will. He was not interested in throwing back the rope from the ground. He dusted himself with the mud. He applied mud generously on his palms, shoulders, and chest. He started clambering up the wall as if he was the master of the iguana. He had light feet and he clung on to the water pipes without resting his complete weight on them and nimbly found footholds, cringed his body and quickly climbed the steep wall and reached the third floor in a jiffy.

He broke the lock of the door in the fifth room of the safe-keeping warehouse. A lot of sacks were stocked in the loft of the room. He quickly climbed up and inspected. The sacks had the Zamindar household's clothes, jewellery, accessories, and perfumes. Tucked away deep inside was a dusty bundle that was placed upside down. Aanachathan lifted it, turned it around, and started unknotting the jute string that held it together. He found a lot of *valari*s (boomerangs that were used in ancient battles for protecting cattle from predators and for hunting) in it. One particular *valari* had an ivory handle. Aanachathan held it, stroked it and left it back in the bundle.

'When the Britishers laid down a rule that the general public must not carry any weapons, our village elders collected all of these and bundled them up and kept them safely. An official called Robert came and attacked our people with an army and took away all their weapons. Today the same British man has joined hands with other community people and has instigated them to chase us away from this zilla.... they are creating a riot for it. They are the ones responsible for snatching away our weapons and now they are the ones who are compelling us to resort to weapons!'

Aanachathan tied the bundle back and started bringing it down and while climbing down he shared these stories with Valiyan and Chinnasami.

The three of them carried the *valari* bundle and stepped out of the Agraharam, gingerly. Just then Valiyan's sharp knife scraped against a lantern. The guards heard the noise and started chasing Aana's team. The thefts were normally planned with two swift runners, one who led in the front and one who closed the line. Aanachathan and Chinnasami were good as lead runners, while Valiyan was good at chasing someone and closing the line. Aanachathan was well aware of this and so did not give any other responsibility to Valiyan, other than chasing. 'You just keep running, Valiya,' is all Aanachathan said and he ran along with Chinnasami and used the slingshot to hit the chasers with pebbles. Aanachathan was talented in taking aim and firing the pebbles with great force.

Many of the chasing guards halted because they were hit by the pebbles. But one group was relentlessly chasing him. Aanachathan stamped on something midway. He took a fraction of a second to take a closer look at it. It was a tiny rat snake. He picked it up, coiled it and fired it through the slingshot. When the guards realised they were being attacked by a snake, they split and scattered away and ran for dear life. Then he tore the country rope into pieces and shot each piece through the slingshot. The petrified guards presumed the pieces of rope to be snakes and moved away in panic.

The chasing dogs neared their targets and were about to clamp their jaws onto them. Chinnasami threw the marijuana balls at them. The dogs chewed on them and felt faint and high and lay down near the shrubs.

Aana's team crossed the third Vandipettai and slithered into the thorny forest. The chasing guards who carried rifles took a potshot at them. Chinnasami defended himself from the flying bullet by using his spear to ward it off. One of the bullets whizzed past Aanachathan's dhoti and the marinated and dried short eats and onion balls scattered around. The next bullet hit his shoulder. The next second the three of them vanished from sight. The rifle troop was confused and, not knowing which side to move, they went back. Midway in the forest, Aanachathan instructed Valiyan and Chinnasami not to follow him. With the bullet wound on his left shoulder and the *valari* bundle on his right, he trudged all night through the forest and reached the banyan tree of Kalappanpatti.

00000000002

Nithilan's iPhone 23 had been charged up to 100 per cent and was ready for use. But this dawn, he didn't bother with it. Right from the time he woke up, he had been squeezing his last bit of energy into making lemon rice. Every time he tossed the rice in the pan, a flavourful aroma arose out of it, and Nithilan was enjoying it with his eyes closed. He did not shy away from smiling at himself and expressing his joy. His sheer pleasure in cooking was to find this special smile. His very calmness reflected in dicing potatoes into perfect small circles, ready to be fried.

Green, red, yellow, purple—about seven to eight lunch baskets were carrying the names of the students in their underbelly as Akash, Sathana, Buvanesh, etc. Sharp at eight the mothers and their children will ring Nithilan's doorbell one after the other and the baskets will be handed over one after the other. Nithilan stayed in Ananda Flats, Nungambakkam, and he had personally requested this part-time job of packing lunch for the school-going kids in his apartment. On the advice of his doctor, he had taken some conscious measures to detox from his arduous computer-based work and this was one such initiative.

He had been reading all night about Orgs, a software that researches the Internet traffic and had been up all night to retrieve the data that had been stolen and had hit the sack at five in the morning. As far as his full-time job was concerned Nithilan was on a mountain; at times he became one.

Sirrius company was involved in creating 'Adayal,' a common scheme, which would create a citizenship number for every Indian. It was a far-sighted job by the agency and it was creating the complete technology to enable this process. The process of enrolling members, doing authentic verification and the building of infrastructure had been completed. Hundreds of employees and thousands of fieldworkers had been working on this project. Nithilan was a vulnerability analyst in the data protection department of Sirrius. He was tagged as 'vulner' Nithi and many claimed the tag was given because of his specialised skills.

Nithilan had very specialised responsibilities:

- To create and customise computer systems based on the requirements of the big data centre
- Entry and accessibility arrangements had to be designed
- Data encryption
- To monitor all the net connections of the centre and to observe unauthorised entries if any
- To check the protection and maintenance arrangement; to research if there had been any 'SQL' injections
- To create a dossier of security suggestions that the organisation and employees must follow and to train the employees to follow the security procedures
- To do interactive tests in the computer and net connections for security breaches and to check the security of all the computers in the workstations in the organisation.

Nithilan was a modern security officer for the Indian big data centre. If Nithilan did enter politics, he would be acclaimed as 'the commander-in-chief of the Indian citizens' biometrics data protection army,' but of course, he wouldn't enter politics.

Nithilan was a native of Natham. But for the past four to five generations, his family had been born and raised in Chennai. The rise and fall of his clan had been out of Chennai. Pramil Swaminathan, his project director, would call him 'Natham Nithilan'. Pramil's liking for Nithilan might be questionable but he liked the ring that the tag had.

His parents had gone back to the ancestral lands to do farming. Once a week he met them on a video call but then he would be busy with other chores even after the call went through and would personally disconnect himself from the call very soon. He would clear his messy desk and wipe it free of every speck only then. He would riffle through the pages of the book that he had bought eons ago. He would contemplate the gifts given to him by Senga and mentally run through which to retain and which to toss. Unmindful of his antics, Nallachamy and Parameswari would recount all the anecdotes of the village, the realities of farming conditions, and pour out to their hearts' content and flap around the video like a bird twittering near the window, and then would vanish when they were done. The one constant request that Nithilan's mom had for him was to shave his beard off.

'Would the world turn a flip and hang upside down if you shave your beard off? Why do you hide your pretty face behind the bush? You are lost in the quagmire of this overgrowth!'

Parameswari did have a point and was certainly stating facts. Nithilan did not fit the bill of a conventionally handsome man as viewed by the rest of the world. He was of average height, had a slight emerging paunch, eyes were sharp and small like grains, and sported coarse thick hair that was bushy and wild and didn't need combing; a dark two-month-old beard was a constant. But what stood apart from all of this was his overwhelming passion that was on a constant search and this added fire to his personality. This fire burned bright not only on his face but even his beard stood aglow. He might either be seeking professionally or he may be getting lost in the depths of his love for Senganthal. Seeking and losing are the same events in love, right?

'Yesterday, the ginger chicken you made was amazing, Nithilan. Thank you.'

Akash's mother Manjula, who had come to collect her son's

lunch basket, expressed her preference for Nithilan beyond his professional service of making lunch. Nithilan noticed the flirty nuance in Manjula's tone and decided to acknowledge it by a fraction of a smile.

Pramil Swaminathan called him the second time.

'Is it true, Nithi?'

'Yes, sir. A person's Adayal data had been sold in WhatsApp for a pittance of ₹500.'

'Disastrous!'

'Our PR team struggled very hard to keep it away from the press, but it has been leaked on a couple of YouTube channels. These would spread and procreate for a week and die a natural death.'

'I know, Nithi. We have a meeting with the CEO, at 10 in the morning. Come prepared with a report.'

'Done, sir.'

000000000003

A ball that glowed dark brown slipped from the experimental apparatus and rolled on the floor. It looked like the nest of a weaverbird, compressed into a 'laddu'. One would know that it was a ball of root, only upon closer inspection. It rolled in its rhythm as if it were chanting the name of its motherland. The research assistant ran behind it and picked it and fixed it back in the apparatus and the 'root ball's' various properties were tested. An elderly man, the director of the lab, who had the appearance of the Mahabharata's character Shakuni, was making notes about the root in his computer.

Linga, the secretary of the Central Home Ministry, and some higher police officials were seated outside the glass walls of the lab and were watching the proceedings of the lab on the screen. They all had an intense expression of anticipation in their eyes. The average temperature of the room soared due to their anxiety. The elderly man shared some details on the mike with Linga.

'The modulus of rupture is good, compressive strength is within the normal range—,' he went on explaining the characteristics and the properties of the root, and just then,

'Sir, no one is going to build a hut out of it. If you could please test our requirements and let us know, that would do!'

The elderly man did not enjoy this sudden interruption of the home ministry's secretary. There was a silence for five seconds. That represented his anger. The elderly man sent the various details that he had documented on his computer as a mail to the secretary.

He barked 'mail' into the mike and started munching on the apple pieces that he had brought along.

Secretary Linga, opened his email and read the details of the lab report completely. At the end of the report was the result, 'extreme match,' and this brought delight to him. The second part of the report elaborated on the significance of the root and detailed diagrams of its far-sighted uses and benefits. As the root came from the catali plant the elderly man had baptised the root ball as 'catalium'.

'The root carries the name of the plant, right? Can't we just call it catali? Why have a new name?' Linga enquired over the mike. The elderly man took his own sweet time to respond and munched over five pieces of apple calmly.

'If you want to retain the root as it is, then catali would suffice, but then it is going to be a raw material for something else. A being or thing needs a name beyond its culture, for the purpose that it is used.'

Having answered the question, he picked the last piece of apple and offered it to Linga.

Linga politely declined and smiled.

'Would you accept a bitten apple, only from Steve Jobs?'

Linga did not have the luxury of time to retort to the elderly man's query. He shared his email with the Home Ministry and the Prime Minister's Office (PMO).

Forty-five-year-old Linga had a salt-and-pepper beard. The grey in his beard was faint and speckled like the raindrops clinging to the grill of a window. He had bagged a doctorate for his research on 'Alternate Communications' from the IIT Madras. Despite his busy schedule with the Home Ministry, his hobby was to understand the various new technological innovations in the field of communication and patent them in his name.

On his way from the Real Earth Research Centre to the restaurant at the Paranthe Wali Gali, Old Delhi, he saw some pigeons by the side of the road.

'Hey…hold on!'

When the driver applied a sudden break, half the pigeons flew away.

Linga stepped down stealthily and stood with his hands tied in his front and observed their tail track quietly. He was looking at them keenly till they flew away. He made some notes on his mobile phone and picked a couple of feathers that were strewn on the ground.

At the restaurant, he had ordered for *rabdi parantha*. By the time the milk within the parantha started leaking on the plate, Linga received a call from the minister. He ordered *rabdi parantha* for the minister too.

'Sir, did you see the report?'

'Catalium?'

'Yes, sir.'

'Good name.'

Linga smiled.

'It's a great news for the nation.'

'Absolutely, sir.'

'Come to the restaurant.'

'On the way, sir.'

Linga stepped out, armed with another *rabdi parantha*.

Everyone was wearing dark glasses in that city. One needed to ask the question 'why' only to Mohan Janarthanan. It was a virtual world that he had created in the Meetaverse, a 3D website through his creative imagination. Just as an author creates a character resembling himself in his writing, there was a 'mirror' representing Mohan himself in his imaginary world. His replica lived in that world and was involved in the development of that city. Mohan would mirror his friends too in the computer world. Each of them would join in that world from their respective accounts. Yesterday he had created a new kind of animal in that world. It had water nails—a flume of water flowed from the place where the nails were supposed to be. It would keep the city and the surroundings wet constantly. Before he could decide whether it was a house pet or a wild animal, he was swamped by his office work. The decision was still left hanging there. He removed his augmented reality headset around midnight. The head of Sirrius cannot live in a shadow world for long.

Mohan Janarthanan was so imposingly tall that it looked as if another man was standing on his shoulders. He had a golden baldness, ideal for an industrialist. His moustache kind of never sprouted. But he sported a luxuriant moustache for his virtual Meetaverse mirror. He had an ideally presentable camera-friendly face, that could feature in any magazine cover, in an instant. He had authored books on modern India and future technologies and they had been prescribed at universities as academic texts. His birth certificate claimed his age as fifty-five. 'I am always a twenty-one-year-old fool with no future,' was his self-declared statement. He did not miss his Palmgrove Hotel coffee on his way to Sirrius's office from his Poes Garden house. Old man

Ramakrishnan, donned in khaki uniform, would spill an ancient pre-Independent era smile at Mohan and used to welcome him when he saw him in the restaurant. Mohan would be receiving a call very soon, in an hour from the PMO and yet Mohan did not transfer that anxiety and adrenalin to his coffee; he sipped it calmly. As he got to the last drop of coffee in the mug, his mind flew to his office.

'In 2018, nearly 200 government websites made Adayal's details public by leaking them. It became accessible to everyone. The departments did this unknowingly. When they were pottering around some other access means, the Adayal Kiosk opened accidentally as the Adayal number is linked with a PAN card and driving license. Similarly, 5,000 government staff were able to have access to Adayal data. We followed your advice and blocked the rights of access to all of them and that's how we set it right. But none expected yesterday's debacle.'

Pramil Swaminathan, director of Adayal, Sirrius, was speaking in a low tone with a bent head; Mohan Janarthanan stared at him unblinkingly. Many important officials were present in the room with folded hands.

'They have sold a citizen's Adayal details for a mere ₹500. Had they at least priced it at ₹1,000, it would have been respectful to the endeavours we have taken for that.'

Pramil knew that it was not sarcasm but anger on Mohan's part to have made this statement. The rest of the team was also quite aware of it. Everyone was expecting some form of apology.

'In India, specifically, the poor people seem to get lost without any identity when they move from one state to another or one city to another. In our country, whichever organisation the poor approach, they are plagued with questions about documents, instructed to fill forms that they don't comprehend, and are intimidated by overwhelming documentation and they are kept in that state of threat; the Adayal has been a good solution for them. For the world to believe that he is a citizen, his credibility is in this one number. This one number can fetch him all the benefits that the nation gives him through various schemes. What else can give you greater pride in this lifetime than protecting the dignity of such a scheme? What else can be your job?'

Mohan scanned all the eyes in the room and none had a response.

'How did this happen, Pramil?'

'Sir looks like the hand of a regular data sweeper. At the time of the customer's usage, data gets decrypted for a microsecond. The very next second it gets encrypted. They have created malware to sweep that data in that interval and have stolen the data.'

'Pramil, there are thousands of thieves in cyberspace. More will come. It's not our job to catch the thieves. Our job is to protect and secure the house. We have to lock and secure the house safely. We should ensure that outsiders cannot have access to the house without the help of the people at home. Security measures need to be strengthened. I will not burden you with the pressures I get from the top level. But you must be cognizant of your pressures.'

'Yes, sir. But for our vulnerability analyst Nithilan's intervention, we could not have arrested the leak, yesterday, sir.'

'Yes, I noticed. He had written a killware against that malware, overnight corrupted the hacker's system, and even identified the hacker for us. Great news!'

There was a power outage just then.

'Sir, it appears that we are the only ones affected by the outage.'

'I guess the smart grid power sources must have failed. Ask them to change it to regular sources.'

'Sir....'

'Is Nithi in the cabin?'

Pramil called Nithi on his mobile.

'He is at the parking, sir. Shall I ask him to come?'

Mohan nodded his head in the affirmative and opened the windows. The smart grid electrical infrastructure, which was right outside the window, looked like a colossal carcass.

A tunnel camp was constructed at Sanjay Van in Old Delhi.

In this industrial expanse which stretched for about a few acres, there were many small rooms, and spare parts were being manufactured in many of these rooms. Right at the centre was stationed a blue colossus.

One cannot call it a train; it looked like many blue spaceships, that were interlinked with one another. A person who sees them cannot name them immediately. But those working in the camp referred to it as a train. The government called it 'Veer Jadayu,' and the spaceships glowed blue in the middle, but still the employees and officials in the camp did not get used to the name.

The Home Minister Rajkumar, the Defence Minister Bahadur Shah, the Principal Secretary of the Armed Forces Govardhan Sarkar and Para Commando Special Officer Nisha Pilot had all gathered at the centre. Many of the employees and workers at the industrial centre were Tamils and hence when the Home Minister arrived there, a *Thirukural* was stammered into the mike by him. The employees would plaster a smile on their faces apologise to Thiruvalluvar in their minds and continue with their jobs. The Home Minister's grandson Sourav who had accompanied him, threw a tantrum because he did not understand the *Kural* and wanted to know its meaning. His grandfather drew a blank. 'It is the military's secret,' said Govardhan and effectively shut his mouth.

Home Secretary Linga entered the camp with his *rabdi parantha* parcel. The moment Sourav sniffed its aroma he went and grabbed the parcel from Linga's hands. He finished it in three ravenous bites. The home minister who was salivating for a piece of it, was left with nothing.

The Chief Engineer Jaishankar took the whole group in a procession. He showed them around 'Veer Jadayu' which had been installed based on a GO, and explained the process that had been set up until then and brought the group up to date. Each ship was called a pocket and there were twelve pockets. Jaishankar announced that the first pocket was ready for experiment and promised to show it was working completely in a day or two.

'So, don't we have the test run today?' the Home Minister's disappointment was loud and clear.

'There is a small glitch in the entropy machine, sir. It has been fixed. Still, we don't want to risk it with you, today. We wanted to do a few test-runs amongst ourselves and then inform you....'

'Linga, at what level is your 'Atharvana' radio?' enquired Govardhan.

'We shall show you a demo day after tomorrow, sir.'

Nisha Pilot's eyes suddenly started screening the spaceship anxiously.

'What is it, Nisha?' asked a concerned Govardhan.

'Sourav?' Nisha started scoping to her right and left.

The Home Minister's grandson Sourav was not found anywhere at that camp level. The whole commando troop scattered in search of the grandson. The Home Minister was worried and anxious. To everyone's surprise and shock, 'Veer Jadayu's' first pocket started moving. Sourav waved his hand and smiled through the glass of the pocket. Jaishankar was stunned.

When the assistant engineer's team was testing the first pocket Sourav had inadvertently got into the first pocket. The pocket had started moving. It entered hyperbolic pipe-like rails.

'Sourav...!' cried the minister and tried to run to the rails. The rest stopped him from approaching closer. Jaishankar picked up his walkie-talkie and spoke to the assistant engineers' team...

'Stop the run...now...a boy is inside....do you hear...

anyone?'

There was a fault in the communication.

Nisha Pilot, unmindful of all the instructions around her ran towards the rail pocket in a great rush. It entered a cave. She jumped into the pocket. She broke the glass window and entered. After that, the pocket vanished from sight. None of the computers in that experimental lab had any blip of the path of the pocket. Jaishankar ran into the security area and adjusted the measures of all the equipment in the blink of an eye. Slowly the pocket started reappearing from the cave to the centre. The minister and the officials anxiously moved closer to the pocket and observed Nisha carrying Sourav on her shoulder and she jumped out of the pocket. Sourav had fainted. Sourav and Nisha carried some burn injuries on their bodies.

The first aid crew arrived promptly and treated Sourav. He gained consciousness.

'Village…....fire…dead bodies…' Sourav babbled something like a nightmare and started screaming. The minister embraced his grandson to his chest. Nisha Pilot had some scratches on her face. The first-aid crew treated her back and hip by applying medications and inspected her for any cracks in the bones. Jaishankar came running out of the security room to report the incident. Employees from various levels had also gathered at the centre.

'If you wrongly quote the *Kural*, this is what will happen,' one of the employees commented. Nisha Pilot heard him muttering. She turned around and glared at the group from where the comment had emanated. At least ten of the employees started sweating in fear of her reprimand.

As soon as you enter the Sirrius office complex, right behind the security cell, you will find a huge neem tree. Nithilan had a habit of sitting under the tree and sipping his first cup of tea before he went into the office to start his work. He didn't have time for his pet peeve that day because he had a meeting with the CEO. The day started without the neem tree.

By the time he reached Mohan Janarthanan's office on the fifth floor, Nithilan kept hearing the whining of 'server down,' 'signal drop,' and 'network jam,' complaints belonging to the same family of issues.

Mohan Janarthanan had a heated conversation with the PMO, about the leakage of information regarding Adayal and had retreated into his Meetaverse to cool off by watering the lawns in his city. The creature that he had formed was licking Mohan's mirror character.

'Why is everyone wearing dark glasses in your Meetaverse, sir?'

After asking the question, Nithilan was staring at the Meetaverse City on Mohan's big exposed computer screen. Mohan lifted his augmented reality glasses and looked at Nithilan.

'Is it that important now, Nithi?'

'Sorry, sir.'

'Yesterday, you had counter-attacked the hacker at the right time. Good job! But do remember the blunder is larger than the fix.'

'I agree, sir. I have reduced the delay in the decryption, sir. I have developed new keys. I have sent a mail for your approval. Such a thing is not likely to happen in the future.'

'Never shall it happen ever, is like a divine ordain. We can't afford to talk like the gods. We shall address it when it happens. I have called you here today not to address this. I have assigned a new task for you. It is regarding the "Double Red" operation of the Home Ministry. Of course, it is strictly confidential. Other than you, me, and Pramil, nobody else in the office knows about it and I prefer it to stay that way.'

'Sir.'

'You need to design a mini container box. We are going to stack root balls, the size of stress balls. A box must contain a minimum of a hundred balls. Significantly, the box's lock must be hard to crack. Pramil will give you the details of the specifications and dimensions of the box.'

It was hardly ever easy for Nithilan to spout 'Yes, sir.'

'What root is that, sir? May I know?'

'Catalium.'

'Do I have a deadline?'

'Ten working days.'

'Ten might be a little too....'

'Long! Do you have any further questions? If you do, don't waste my time asking them. Get to work.'

'Sir.'

Mohan turned his attention to his computer. Nithilan got up and gathered his shoulder bag. While he walked to the door...

'Nithi, have you watched old movies like *Pathala Bairavi* or *Maya Mothiram?*'

Nithilan understood the question but could not fathom the purpose of the question and hence stood there staring.

'I have seen them when young. But I don't remember any of them now.'

'How about *Harry Potter* and *Star Wars?*'

'I have read the books on Harry Potter, but otherwise....'

'Have you ever wondered why those worlds are interesting

and ours is dull and boring?'

'No, sir. I find our world in itself quite interesting. I am not able to handle this "interest factor" sufficiently.'

'Ha, ha!'

Those who looked into Nithilan's cabin found him seated there bereft of his signatory tea and threw him a look of pity. Everyone knew that other than tea, nothing or none was his companion in the office. He was highly respected at his workplace. But he never overstepped the line of respect and made any intimate friends with anyone. Rakesh, Mustafa, and Tamilselvi were his teammates and showed genuine interest in befriending him, but he maintained a distance and did only lip service to his acquaintances, blaming it on the burden of his work. At times his colleagues would murmur that he was arrogant, behind his back. This society could handle chatterboxes but didn't know what to do with the silent ones!

He sat under the neem tree with his laptop during lunch hours. He was reading the journals on 'complex locker systems'. A tender young branch of the tree bent towards him. It was dancing around him as if it had saved a kiss for him. His morning trip to Mohan Janarthanan's room was like a journey into the never-ending spiral-like *Kanni Theevu* (a popular comic strip in a Tamil daily) where he had been assigned to run the errand of buying vegetables! It was truly a strange experience. Nithilan could not figure out Mohan's urgency and his questions. Nithilan pondered over the connection between the container box that he was asked to design and the *Pathala Bairavi* movie. A crow plopped its shit right on Nithilan and his pondering!

Nithilan generally chilled out in two ways. One was having his tea under the neem tree. The other was listening to a song from the old Tamil movie *Maya Bazaar*, *'Thangame, un pola thanga padhumai engengu thediyum, yaarumillai.'* [Golden girl, I am unable to find a golden doll like you anywhere] The introduction of the song was picturised with actors Savitri and Thangavelu laughing loudly, one after the other, and Nithilan enjoyed that hilarity. Towards the end of the song, Thangavelu would clap his hands and sing along and Savitri would use her magic to get his palms plastered and this made Nithilan burst into peals of laughter. That day his mind was quite anxious to meet his golden girl Senganthal.

Senga's unique quality was that she would make a lot of effort to verify the information that she received to authenticate it. Yet, Nithilan would fondly call her a 'WhatsApp forward'. He enjoyed the annoyance he caused her by using that tag.

Adayal details had leaked and Senga alias Seganthal released a video of it on her YouTube channel named *Sirupillaithanam* (Childishness). Nithilan tried hard to dissuade her but she would not relent. According to her, 'Vulner' Nithilan and her lover Nithilan were two different species. Her video was removed because it did not adhere to the stipulated social media rules, and the Ministry of Information and Broadcasting had issued her a warning.

'What does this "Jelly" mean?'

Nithilan found it to be a new word. Nithilan was riffling through Senga's written scripts for the video to be recorded in the recording studio.

'Learn by watching the video.'

She was intensely focussing on her hairstyle. Senga was like a black-and-white version of the yesteryear actress Jamuna; she was like a beautiful fallacy of Jamuna's portrait. Even in pitch darkness, there would be a ray of glow on her face.

The moment her assistant shouted 'Action', Senga started to talk.

Nithilan was capturing his favourite angle of Senga's photograph on his phone.

'The New World Technology group had issued a report last week. I am not sure as to how many of you have seen it. Just as the coronavirus consumed human bodies, our whole digital world is likely to be consumed by this virus called Jelly and bring it to a standstill. Yes! Absolute fact! The name is sweet alright but it is a devil that is going to take us back to the stone age.

'Our mobile phones, computers, traffic system, smart grid power, banking system—you name it, everything is going to freeze. This is what is anticipated. Technological lifestyle based on computers might vanish. The whole data of this world can get corrupted. No one has tracked the origin of the Jelly virus yet. But I have a question. People who are adamant about converting everything into the digital form, people who spend millions for advertising and advocating, 'go digital,' have they thought of protecting this digital world in any way? I don't know!'

Nithilan felt that she was talking the usual doomsday speech, characteristic of the social media world. Nithilan did not relish Senga's speech half as much as he relished her lips.

'Are we ready for a digital apocalypse? Viewers comment on this. We shall talk about this in detail in the next video.'

Nithilan enjoyed the choice of words: Digital apocalypse.

'Just because you want to increase the number of views, you are stating things out of the blue! 'Digital apocalypse,' huh? Your choice of words is interesting indeed!'

Senga was busy in the kitchen in her apartment right above the studio, cooking for Nithilan. She was making rotis. He was marinating chilli chicken with spices.

'Is it wrong to point out a mistake? My video on Adayal leakage has been removed because of the pressures that your department used. They have even issued a warning. Do inform them that I am shivering in my boots...hmph!!'

'Senga, I told you so. These are not the stuff in which you should be involving yourself. Without any reason....'

'What? Without any reason, countless number of people have trusted their personal data under your care. Are they not visible enough to you? Their voiceless plea is not a good enough reason for you?'

'Our citizens can move to any corner of the country and can still claim the benefits given to them through the various schemes under the government without struggling under a paper mound of documentation. One Adayal would suffice. Adayal is the digital umbilical cord that links our government to an individual citizen. What a grand progress, huh?'

'Didn't we see the apathy of selling one umbilical cord for ₹500? I bet you want to change this nation into a surveillance state. You want to monitor everyone. You don't like anyone raising a question. You play different designs of democratic games to ensure your objective. The umbilical cord, my foot…'

'Look here. Every system is likely to have a problem. It takes time to settle down and it is a gradual progress. Every policy will have its share of good and bad. Your social media is a negative one. It's a mega dump yard. When you stand over the dump and survey, all that you see around you would be nothing but rubbish.'

'Social media is not a negative media. It's as real as any media. I enjoy being a dustbin, I prefer it over being a flower pot. Let me be!'

'Mmmm…. only God can save you.'

'We need to save that God from all of you, right away.'

'Are you ridiculing my faith in God?'

'I too have faith you fool! The God within me is peaceful but you hand weapons to him and make him a tyrant. I don't approve of that. That too, you do it on the sly, without my permission!'

'Silly! If it is peaceful, it's no God but a mere stone!'

'You give this grand talk as if you have played kabaddi with God. Stop now and get the chicken boiled.'

'I understand that the chicken has no mood to be cooked.'

Nithilan always looked at her bristling anger as an opportunity to envelop her in a hug. He would start as softly as a stroke of a peacock feather and then fit her into a tight, breathless hug and move around; she started screaming, 'Leave me…' and in that struggle, she missed her balance and fell on the living room couch.

'Hey…the roti on the tava….'

She tried to escape his clutches and Nithilan chose the moment to kiss her hard on her lips. Her top and short skirt seemed to oblige him and moved and gave way to his caress. Nithilan's soft and hard caresses seduced Senga and her eyes closed in appreciation. Soon enough the clothes that were in the way were removed and thrown far away. Nithilan pressed his lips below Senga's navel and moved his lips up and down. She loved to tease him and see his pangs. Government, Adayal, people, and the disjointed conversation were discarded like the marinated chilli chicken.

Nithilan was drinking in the dew drops of sweat on Senga's back in an absorbed manner. Finally, through the daze of his mind, he heard the ring of the tenth call that came to his mobile. Nithilan rose slowly, carefully ensuring that the smell of Senga's sexual craving did not fritter away from his body and checked his mobile. The call was from Mohan Janarthanan. He was not the tenth caller—he had been the one who had called ten times!

John the Ripper had declared that it was because of a weak password. Splunk suspected that network morphing might have happened. Just when Nithilan carried this report to Mohan's room, he found Home Ministry's Secretary Linga talking intensely with Pramil Swaminathan, the director of the Adayal division. Linga pointed out to a bird in the computer and Pramil was listening to Linga's side of the story without the blink of an eyelid.

'I called you several times, and you did not attend. What exactly were you up to?'

Mohan Janarthanan asked a pointed question and Nithilan managed to fend it off with a feeble lie. Mohan Janarthanan chose to pass the lie dipped in lusty naughtiness.

Two days back, a specific voice file had been stolen from the Indian army. The Indian Home Ministry perceived it to be the job of the Chinese government's Internet spies. If only they could identify the measures adapted to steal the files, then they could also protect them and ensure that such a theft did not happen in the future was what the defence and home ministries believed. They were driving the specialists of their respective cyber units crazy. The Home Minister Rajkumar had sought the help of his friend Mohan Janarthanan. Mohan had handed over the task to Nithilan. Since the early dawn, Nithilan has worked on various softwares and experimented in many ways.

'The password had been very weak, sir. They had used it for network morphing.'

'Network morphing, huh?'

'Yes, sir. They had created a fake network just like ours and have rerouted the data that they wanted through it. The rest of the details are in this report, sir.'

'Thank you, Nithi.'

'Sir…'

'Yes, go on.'

'The audio clip had two words that were used frequently, "catalium" and "Jadayu". It was a Hindi clip and I didn't understand much. Is it the same catalium that we talked about?'

'Yes.'

'Jadayu?'

'Did I not ask you to design the container box? How much have you progressed?'

'I am creating a locker code for the box, sir. Pramil has given me the physical parameters for the box. The design is ongoing. They have promised to deliver the alpha model tonight.'

'It should be resistant to winds, rains, cyclones, and erosion.'

'Yes, sir.'

'Let me know when the model is ready. We shall meet then.'

'Sir.'

Nithilan was standing directly opposite Sirrius's office in a snack bar, called 'Nagathaal Bajji,' and he noticed the Home Ministry's Secretary Linga's car speeding out of Sirrius.

Nithilan screwed his eyes to observe if Pramil Swaminathan was hanging on to the rear side of the car. Pramil was quite capable of hanging out but then he wasn't to be found.

Nithilan was daydreaming about Noah's ship, getting geared somewhere. The oil in the bajji was so sticky that it smeared an oily sheen onto his dream and the ship glimmered with an oily surface. Wind, rains, cyclones, and erosion, Mohan's intimidating vocabulary list must have rubbed off into his dream too.

'It doesn't work, sir. When I reached out to customer care, they said that they do not know how long it would take.'

Nithilan always used to pay through Paytm in the snack bar. He spilled all the coins that he had in his wallet onto the lid of the butter biscuit jar. The coins clinked with a loud noise, rolled over and stood still peacefully. The shopkeeper gathered every coin without leaving behind any. Nithilan just stood there. The shopkeeper realised a trifle late that he had gathered two extra rupees and thrust two faded orange candies into Nithilan's hands.

'Sir, isn't he Home Ministry's Secretary, Linga?' he questioned Pramil who later joined him.

Nithilan felt that his head would burst if he did not get to know about the meeting between Pramil and Linga. But he knew he could not appease Pramil with a cheap bribe of two faded orange candies.

'He was talking to me about his new project and I too gave him some input.'

Nithilan felt like grabbing the orange candy from his mouth and feeding it to the strays. As soon as he found his seat back in his cabin, he found a notification that the alpha model of the container had been sent to his email. The containers were orange too!

Holes had been made inside the box to safely store the catalium balls. The edges were made out of bamboo-pulp mould. The outside of the box had a layer of goat's skin mixed with iron dust and hence it was sturdy. As per Nithilan's notes and directions, the front portion of the box had three holes, the size of chalk pieces, and convex mirrors were placed on them. A provision for inserting a microchip had been provided on the right. On the top, a matchbox-sized visual screen was placed. The designers of the box had also sent a short film on the graphical design of the box. In the video, one could see the box from various angles as the box rolled, turned, opened, shut, got knocked on the floor, floated on the water, got clawed by animals, got nibbled and chewed by animals, got stamped by dinosaurs, hit by elephants, attacked by thunder and lightning and without getting affected or dented it jumped on to its throne like a saffron-coloured calf and started trumpeting its glory. All it missed was an ad jingle behind like: *colour, quality, permanence.* Nithilan enjoyed the advertisement graphics more than the design of the box.

'Shall we go on a *Una*?'

The journey of going to many restaurants in the day or the evening and raiding them for food had been creatively coined in Tamil by Senga as Una. It was a private code between the couple. When Nithilan saw her text, he started getting hunger pangs right away.

It was the month of Ramzan. *Iftar* food filled the air with its appetising aroma. They chose the Mannadi streets for their Una. They got into the metro train and while on the journey, Nithilan was caught up with the locker system and the Python program he was writing for it.

Aagol | 45

Senganthal snapped his attention from his thought cloud.

'Are you pining for all the lost love that you had during your college days?'

He smiled.

'My friend Mathura would often say that memory is a nasty prankster.'

'OMG! I assure you I was not thinking of any such thing. I forgot the name of that shop in Mannadi. That is called....'

'Hathim?'

'Yeah.... Hathim...Hathim!'

'You could have asked me that. Then it was something that you cannot talk to me about. Accept the truth.'

'If you keep on prattling nonstop, you and I know exactly where it would lead to. So don't.'

Nithilan smiled shyly.

'This is a public place. You can do nothing to me.'

Even in a public place, her look and tone seemed to invite him to overstep. Just one look cast by Nithilan made her 'nothing' into 'something.' The old man sitting next to them was waiting for a lip-lock scene.

Nithilan held Senga's hand. He interlocked his fingers with hers. He took her thumb very close to his face and gently moved it to the sides. He ran through the lines and mounts with his pointer finger and seemed to make a thorough research.

'You goof! This doesn't seem like romance at all. I think you are caught up with your official work.' She shook her hands off him.

'Well! You seem to have caught on.'

The old man got out of the metro at the next stop feeling disappointed.

'You teased the old geezer and let him down, Nithi. He flew off in a rage!'

Nithilan's favourite Irani malai tandoori had run out in Hathim's shop. Senga's favourite, piping hot Lucknow mutton kebab was available. Keema samosa was as soft as a pillow. The base was as crisp as a dream stuck to the pillow. The two of them were not deterred by their preferences. They raided it and even gave up on the idea of visiting the other restaurants.

A visually challenged woman came to the shop and enquired for a mango pudding. She was wearing dark glasses. Senga picked a mango pudding and showed it to the shopkeeper and handed it over to the woman. The woman thanked her and paid for it. She walked away with the help of her cane. Her black glasses distracted Nithilan and he went off on a spiral of thoughts.

They were ambling along sipping on rose lassi when Senga shook him back to reality.

'How come you have gone all silent?'

'That's nothing. What is the response to your Jelly video?'

Senga split into a lassi-whipped smile spraying lassi around.

'Nithi, our people have learned to live around everything. Nothing will affect them. Whatever happens around us we scamper around like those characters in video games and drop dead. We are just shadow characters. Democracy is failing. This is the time of electoral autocracy. Soon it would evolve as an absolute technocracy. Henceforth there are no people-related issues, only power play.'

'Was the mutton kebab that bad? You seem to be puking words!'

'Your New India brain will treat this as puke, of course.'

The visually challenged woman was sitting at a distance. She was stroking her mobile with her fingers and seemed to be trying to access her bank account. She failed to get the connection. Nithilan was quiet, till they crossed her.

The lollipop looked fluffy, like that of a polar bear's head. It had ears too. It had honied cashew whiskers. It was manufactured in Switzerland's Michigan chocolate factory and about fifty select rich families imported these specialised chocolates in India, including the most popular cocaine lollipop. Mohan Janarthanan's family was one of the fifty rich families to import them.

Machiavelli was determined to have one of the cocaine lollipops even before he could brush his teeth in the morning; he was Mohan Janarthanan's thirteen-year-old son. He had never regretted the fact that he was named after an Italian thinker. It may take some more years for him to understand that Machiavelli was the author of Mohan Janarthanan's favourite political book. Or he may never get there. His friends called him Mac and he liked that name.

After getting a divorce from Mohan, Machiavelli's mother Pushpalatha flew somewhere abroad with her male friend. The court gave Mohan the custody of his son. Machiavelli did not remember the incidents between his parents. His repository of 'touch' memory did not even have a sample of his mother's touch!

Mac was lying on the comfortable peacock feather mattress, sucking the lollipop and playing the 'League of Legends' on his mobile. He would check out Mohan through his peripheral vision; Mohan, who was seated at a distance was busy building his Meetaverse City on his laptop. Machiavelli would also be roaming as a mirror in the city. That day Mohan was constructing border walls for his city. About 200 virtual employees were sweating over the construction. For every sweat drop the employee would get additional points. But a sweat drop would appear only after he completed the chore. In that virtual world, the bosses decide when and how much their employees should sweat! To refresh the weary workers, a distant waterfall from the mountains would send a misty spray, on and off.

While he was raising the wall, Mohan was also painting pictures on them. As he created the painting of a monstrous mammoth on the wall, he was also checking on Machiavelli. Mac did not remove his lollipop from his mouth and flashed a skewed smile with a cheek puffed up like a balloon.

Mac would always take up Karen as his identity to play the League of Legends game on his mobile. He would take Karen through the arrow-marked path. Karen's sword and the armour on her shoulder would glow like blue beads and this pleased Mac.

'What shall we have for breakfast?'

He did not respond.

'Fruit loops? Bread and omelet….? Dosa…?'

He showed two fingers.

'Did we not have bread and omelet yesterday? Do you want it again?'

He crinkled his eyebrows. Just then Mohan rose from his seat with a jerk as if he underwent an electric shock. A mouse brushed his feet and scurried into the blue carpet to hide. Mohan lifted and shook the carpet. The mouse scampered onto the chair.

Mohan brought a broomstick to chase the mouse. The mouse leaped from the chair onto the bed and jumped onto Machiavelli's tummy. Mohan got anxious. Mac was playing on his mobile imperviously. When the mouse climbed down his legs, it tickled him and Mac tittered. The mouse hid under the peacock feather mattress.

Machiavelli rose slowly and moved to his room. He picked a green knife from his kitchen set of toys. He was still sucking on his lollipop and holding it on one hand he brandished the plastic knife on the other. He kicked the mattress with his leg. The mattress flipped sides. The exposed mouse was running around.

'Hey! That's a toy knife! What are you going to do with that?'

Machiavelli clenched his mobile between his teeth. He leered at the mouse, approached it and with his knife chopped its head in one stroke. The chopped head of the mouse flew in the air, hit the table lamp and fell because of the force he applied. The blood splattered on Mohan's trousers. The brute force that Machiavelli applied to the toy knife entered the mouse's body, sharper than a real knife.

He flipped the peacock feather mattress back to its place, lay down and continued to play his game on the mobile. Mohan removed the mouse's head and body. Machiavelli's blood-stained knife was lying on the floor. Mohan cleaned it and went into the kitchen to make an omelet.

When he poured the first egg to make the omelet, his mobile blipped a notification on important news concerning the laboratory of the Indian Ocean.

00000000011

Adayal Director Pramil was a married man. He and his wife were not interested in having babies. They were of the opinion that all married couples needn't have kids. But now that they had hit their midlife crisis, they felt the emptiness in their lives. In recent days, Pramil's wife Karthika was contemplating about adopting a child. Pramil had discussed this predicament only with Nithilan at work.

Nithilan was seated in his workstation and was busy writing programs for the electronic lock for the catalium box. He had split the lines of the thumb into three parts: first mount, middle mount, and last mount. He had planned to use three people's thumbprints; the first person's first mount of the thumb, the second person's middle mount, and the third person's last mount. Unless the three prints were placed on the box's surface, it would not open. This was the design that he had conceived for the lock. As the prints were placed one after the other, the video screen in the middle of the box would create a form. For the first print, a moustache would appear—for the second print a crown would appear—for the third print a face would appear. It was the image of the Maratha king Chhatrapati Shivaji. If the king's face appeared clearly on the screen, then the box would open. Otherwise, it meant that the wrong prints had been placed. Who were those three men who would offer their thumbprints? Nithilan or Mohan Janarthanan would not choose them. The PMO or the defence secretariat would decide.

'Nithi…you are anyway creating a face…why not actresses like Samantha, Pooja or Kajal Agarwal? Why *Veer* Shivaji?'

When he was testing, Pramil entered the cabin with a few files and asked him with a twinkle in his eye.

Aagol | 51

'You never questioned why the box was in such a flashy recoiling orange colour. When you raised no questions regarding that, then you have no right to question the rest.'

Nithilan had a genuine smile on his lips, a rare sight.

'Without beating around the bush, tell me—I am 45 and my wife Karthika is 42. Should we adopt a child or not?'

'Should you only adopt a child?'

'Why?'

'You see, I am generally free. You can maybe use me…?'

'I asked you not to beat around the bush.'

'Of course, you can adopt. Is forty an age? It is an age when youth tones down a little and gets sculpted into a fine structure. You can adopt as many children as you want. But…'

'But?'

'Let it not be an infant, maybe an eight-year-old or ten-year-old would be better.'

'Why?'

'If you have the dreams of educating the child or getting the child married, then you would get some breathing space for that.'

'You say that the breathing space would not last long?'

'You could say that too.'

'Just now you said that I am at a finely sculpted age.'

'That's true. But who can predict when the next virus attack is likely to happen?'

Pramil smiled.

'That has come already. The digital virus.'

'I don't understand.'

'Did you not watch the news? The digital apocalypse is here. That's the current topic since yesterday.'

The moment Nithilan heard the word digital apocalypse he was stunned and proud at the same time. He was reminded of Senga's prattle and then the bubbles of memory burst. Lost in their intense conversation, Pramil and Nithilan had moved toward the parking lot, opposite the basketball ground. Many senior executives had hit the ground in the name of rejuvenating their tired spirits. They shot the ball everywhere other than the basket and moved all over the ground. The ball seemed exhausted!

'Yesterday, a virus corrupted the systems of the landing stations' cables of the submarine in the Indian Ocean. It was a huge data loss. There was a complete shutdown of the Internet in India and other countries in Asia. They are reviving gradually through satellite alternate methods.'

'Why are we bothering ourselves with under-the-sea Internet? There are a thousand means, through satellite, balloons, and other ways in the air.'

'If you ask me why, I don't have any answers. But then nearly ninety-five per cent of the world's data is transferred by the sea. There are 400 optic fiber cables stretching to seven lakh kilometres. The distance would approximately measure going around the earth thirty-two times. In 1858, Queen Victoria sent a telegraph to the then US President James Buchanan and this was the first ever underwater communication. From then on, till date, every ocean is blended with our talk, our writing, our photographs, our advertisements and our secrets.'

'If we stand on the beach shore and when the waves wet our feet, all we need to do is scoop some foam and it may reveal some truths! Is that what you are saying?'

Pramil smiled.

'But the question in front of us is, who is the person or organisation that controls the submarine cables? In those days the king who conquered many nations was termed as the emperor. Today the one who controls the Internet and the data is the self-proclaimed king.'

'Who is that king?'

'We do not know. The tech giant corporations invest a lot in these cables. One among them must be the king. Air, water, and land are under their control. They term it as 'latency,' i.e., data delay—the time taken for data to move from one point to another. There is a big competition amongst many big giants who are attempting to reduce the delay. Amidst all these dramas someone is intruding with a virus and killing us.'

'Where did this virus come from?'

'Who knows? They have a name……some…'

Nithilan's memory was jogged.

'Jelly?'

'Right…Jelly…Jelly! Look at the way they name it, huh…. Jelly, candy!'

That evening when Nithilan was getting back home, he observed many people complaining that they could not connect to the cell tower. The shops carried 'only cash' boards.

'Your tamarind rice was tasty. I tried to call but did not get any signal.'

Akash's mother Manjula was standing at his doorstep with an Oreo dairy milk chocolate bar in her hand.

'It is Akash's birthday today.'

Nithilan accepted it with a smile. Manjula went about her way—seemingly to get back home. But she seemed anxious to tell Nithilan something before he entered his house. Manjula painstakingly descended every step towards Nithilan's apartment at a snail's-pace like that of a TV serial titled *Bagya*. Nithilan opened his door.

'This black shirt suits you a lot!'

Nithilan looked up and held her eyes in his gaze.

'You could have said that when we met on the ground floor. Did you have to come all the way to say this?'

Manjula dropped a shy smile and rushed up the stairs.

'What? Is it Akash's birthday? Did his mother give you a dairy milk chocolate?'

Senganthal started her inquiry over the mobile.

'What I suggest is that you better go to their house and greet Akash for his birthday. I need to know if it is truly his birthday.'

'You silly girl.'

'Silly, and me? You are the one who is seducing aunties in the guise of making food for their children. Just you wait! When I get hold of you in person, and then…'

'Senga, I have been hearing about your Jelly and the digital apocalypse. It's flashing news!'

'I called you just for that. They have blocked my YouTube channel: *Sirupillaithanam*. I have sent a mail. Your people are the ones who have raised the complaint. It isn't just about me. They have blocked 23 similar YouTubers. They have also made some arrests.'

'Why Senga? You hadn't said anything wrong!'

'I received news about a giant spaceship that is being constructed in Delhi. I had concluded my video with the teaser that we would talk about the spaceship next week.'

'What spaceship?'

'I don't have much news about it. Do you?'

'Senga, why are always targeting government projects for your videos? Please stop. Don't play around with confidential information.'

'Leave that aside. If I get arrested then you must get me out on bail. Don't sit in a corner and chomp on your Oreo dairy milk.'

'Nothing will happen. Be bold!'

Nithilan's daydream of Noah's ship had a rerun in his mind because of Senga's reference.

Mohan Janarthanan, Pramil, and Nithilan placed their thumb impressions together. The box displayed Veer Shivaji's image and it opened. They placed the sample root balls that had been sent to Mohan inside the box and checked the fit. It was perfect!

'I have enabled the network through a chip, sir. Every box is in our network. We can track each one of them. I have used the same algorithm used for our Adayal project, sir.'

'Well done, Nithi! Do we have remote access?'

Nithilan knew quite well that Mohan would address that question.

'No, sir. No one can open the box from the remote, without the physical touch. There are about 2,000 boxes in the design stage. And sir....?'

'Yes, Nithi, shoot.'

'If I know the mode of transport for these boxes, I can design a shield accordingly. How? Where?'

Just at that moment, Machiavelli entered the room unexpectedly. He liked Pramil a lot. He leaned on Pramil's shoulder.

'His school is off for the day. He was bored and so I brought him along.'

No one asked Mohan for an explanation.

Nithilan had heard quite a bit about Machiavelli from Pramil. He apparently did not have a mental growth that matched his age. Nithi met him in person for the first time. Machiavelli smiled at Nithilan. Nithilan stroked his head. Mac immediately slapped Nithilan's hand off. Mac didn't appreciate Nithilan's pity.

'Mac, behave yourself.'

Mohan chided him. He ignored it and sat on Mohan's swivel

chair and went on a spin. Pramil caught on that the chair did not spin as fast as Mac desired. He walked over to Mac with an amiable smile and swung it around. Mac shut his eyes and enjoyed the spin.

'Is Senga your friend?'

The question sent Nithilan on a spin even though he wasn't on a swivel chair.

'Yes...sir...' he muttered.

'Isn't she a popular YouTuber?'

'Is she, sir?'

'What?!'

'Sir, she is a YouTuber alright. But I wouldn't know if she is popular...'

'Five million followers, Nithi! And that's no joke! She must have struggled hard to reach there.'

'Is there any problem, sir?'

'She talks about the highly sensitive projects of the State quite frequently. Linga has put together a list of YouTubers along with the team from the broadcast ministry. They have arrested many of them. As Senga happens to be your friend, they have let her be with just a warning.'

Mac slipped off the swivel chair, lost his balance, and fell to the ground. Pramil rushed to him and lifted him. Mohan picked him up and embraced him close to his chest. Mac did not fight the embrace and stayed in the warmth of it.

'Nithilan, you might have to set off on a journey. I will give the details later.'

Mohan accompanied Machiavelli to the restroom. He cleaned the snot on his nose and washed his face. He removed Mac's shorts and asked him to urinate. He said he didn't want to pee and wore his shorts back. As soon as his shorts were in place, he said he wanted to take a pee!

The usual tea under the neem tree wasn't hot. It had lost its sizzle!

Nithilan wasn't merely an employee of Sirrius, working on the Adayal project. He was also a member of the consultant committee of the IT wing of the ruling government. He influenced the government staff which was just a touch away on his mobile. When he heard that Senga was not arrested because of him he heard the click of a mental salute within him. He kept staring at his image in the mirror. He combed and set his hair but it took longer than usual.

Nithilan couldn't reach Senga. That night Nithilan's mom Parameswari made a video call. 'How is it that your network alone is functional?' he questioned her in frustration. He allowed his mother to go on with her side of the conversation. Her voice was like a soothing lullaby. He fell asleep like a baby. Parameswari was concerned that he might wake up if she stopped talking and so she went on mindlessly. A long while later Senga called. He could read her name off the screen even with his eyes closed.

A band of people were hiding and leaping like a monkey army, weaving their way through the dense mangrove forest. Nisha Pilot was hard on chase and right behind them but missed her gun somewhere inside a hollow tree. She decided that if she tried to search for her gun in the hollow, they might escape and so instead, she pulled out the dagger hidden in her socks. She went on with her chase to attack them.

'East—Southeast...'

She was screaming instructions to her commando troop who were following her, while on the run. The Andaman forests were a strange terrain for Nisha. She believed that we, the people, had the wherewithal to face any forest or mountainous terrain, etched in our DNA over the years of evolution. She would unfailingly teach this faith to her recruits in every class that she taught.

The escaping band came to a screeching halt near a deep ravine. They had no way forward. But Nisha predicted that they would not think twice about jumping into the cavernous ravine to escape or even indulge in mass suicide to evade being caught.

She ordered, 'Pyramid bottom,' to the warriors behind her. Some of the commando troops hunched like cheetahs and jumped into the ravine using ropes aligned like a pyramid and pointed their rifles at the escaping band, stranded on the top.

One from the band pounced to attack Nisha. Nisha placed her left foot on the branch of a tree beside her, leaped, and used her right leg to kick him. He fainted. The rest went down on their knees.

Nisha grabbed the backpack of the man who fainted and opened it. The bag was full of colourful chemicals. There were pieces of equipment used to create the chemicals. They were all wrecked.

'Target captured. Items seized.'

She sent a message to the army secretariat. Nisha asked her commandos to set a camp in the forest. The surrendered band was handcuffed and kept under custody in a separate tent by the commandos.

The neighbouring villages sent provisions for cooking a meal. A campfire was lit in the centre and chicken and fish were fried for dinner.

Nisha and her commando troop were waiting for the chemical expert team of the Real Earth Research Centre. She got information that they had arrived at the Andaman coast.

Early in the dawn, Nithilan woke up to the rain. The clothes that he had hung for drying on the terrace would have gone wet for sure. He was of the attitude that the special feeling of the rains was any day greater than the mundane worries like wet clothes! He had been attempting to move away from the grip of computers and machinery and this therapeutic effort has brought him closer to the wonders of nature. He had started giving the same attention to everything green, just as much as the respect he gave to the neem tree at his office. His schedule stipulated that he spent at least twenty minutes every morning with bird calls. These days he spent nearly thirty minutes on them. He didn't look at them as sounds, he considered them as a presentation made by the skies. That day his skies opened up the rain for him.

He was halfway through getting the lunch boxes ready when he got a ping on his WhatsApp: 'Today is a holiday for schools!' Now, what should he do with all that he cooked? Should he convert the lunch to breakfast? He had nearly two hours before he needed to report to work. Why should his house be quiet and still for the two hours? 'Welcome home for breakfast,' he created a digital invite in seconds and posted it in the Apartment's kids' group. In the next ten minutes, his house was filled. Akash, Sadhana, Buvanesh, Keerthi, Vaibav, Irugesh, Kamal, and Prithvi had all gathered and the food fest started.

'Hey Akash, don't take any more servings of the sambar rice...'

'I took just one serving, okay! Buvanesh dipped his hand into the vessel and ate in kilos!!'

'Keerthi, pass me the papad.'

'Why don't you go and pick your food?'

'How come you cherry-picked all the pink fries?'
'Do you want some, Sadhana?'
'You bit into it. I don't want yours.'
'You are one silly fool!'
'You are calling me names? I am going to complain to Mom.'
'You can even complain to your granny for all I care.'
'Why are you dragging grannies into sambar rice?'
'Granny, granny caught in a trashy cranny!'

Everyone burst out laughing at that gibberish limerick. Outside, the rain lost its battle to the cheer and noise made by the children within!

Akash's mom Manjula entered Nithilan's house armed with a casserole of gulab jamuns. Nithilan protested, 'Why did you take all this effort...?' and unburdened her of the casserole. Everyone present was served a gulab jamun and yet there was enough left to serve a battalion on two other rainy days. The children had thoughtfully carried their toys along. The house which had resembled a food street until minutes ago, suddenly transformed into a gaming hub. No one seemed to be in any kind of urgency to leave. Manjula tried to set right the kitchen which had a 'stormed in' look, thanks to the kids' invasion.

Nithilan had read that the rains always left behind some miracle or the other. He witnessed it in person that day. That morning an additional person rang the doorbell. He opened the door to find Senga standing under an umbrella.

No umbrella can ever win over rain! Her torso and wet clothes were living testimony to that observation.

'Wow! Senga, how come, you are here?'
'Can I come in?'
'Please do.'

Ludo king, football, carrom board, I spy—children had settled for games of their choice. Senga had to wade through the various island settlements of children.

'What is this?'

'School is closed…and so,' he trailed off.

'Since when did you join the school?'

Suddenly from nowhere, a pillow hit Senga's face. She was unnerved for a moment but then she caught up with the momentum and warded it off.

'Keerthi, why did you hit that girl?' Akash sounded excited and anxious.

'Wait! Did he even call me girl?' Senga was baffled.

'Have a gulab jamun,' a woman's voice was heard from behind. Senga turned around to find Manjula standing with a cup.

'Senga, this is Akash, Keerthi, Buvanesh and Irugesh. There are some more kids in the other room. This is Akash's mom Manjula.'

Senga froze like a video that did not have enough signal or net connection.

'Maybe she is way too shy.'

Manjula dumped the cup in Nithilan's hands and went back to the haven of the kitchen.

'Hey Nithi! What exactly is going on?'

'Just a breakfast bash, that's it.'

She picked a gulab jamun from Nithilan's cup and shoved it into her mouth.

'Mmhm… it's super!' She said with a relish and asked, 'Did you make it?'

'It was made by my mom,' chimed Akash immediately in defence of his mom. Senga held Nithilan in a stare.

'She made it for the kids, Senga.'

'Is it expressly written so, on them?'

'Talk softly, you silly! Don't look at everything with jaded eyes.'

'Listen my dear! I am not seeing anything. Nothing at all!'

Nithilan's news channel would run 24/7.

He would not care to watch the news broadcast but still, he was used to having it running in the background.

Senga and Nithilan moved to the balcony. Senga confided in him about the efforts she had taken to keep her YouTube channel up and running and added that she had her channel revived. She also handed over a new shirt that she had bought for Nithilan as a gift. But before handing it over she crushed it and then gave it to him.

'That sister has a crush on our Nithi, I guess,' whispered Akash so loudly that Senga and Nithi laughed at the innocent comment. Keerthi clicked their laughing picture on her mobile.

'You have a mobile for yourself, at this age?' Senga clicked her tongue.

'No auntie. This is my younger sister's phone. Mine is getting charged.'

The children went back to their games.

'Para Commando Special Officer Nisha Pilot has arrested the Chinese terrorists who tried infiltrating the Andamans. Nisha's troops surrounded the terrorists and seized them before they attempted to escape. Some strange chemicals were seized from the terrorists.' This news was seen on the reflection of the balcony window.

'Is she Nisha Pilot?'

Nithilan shifted his eyes from the balcony glass window and looked at the television.

'Why? Do you know her?'

'No! Need to know of her soon.'

'I don't get it.'

'I might have to meet her next week. I have instructions from the office.'

'Be careful my dear! She might book you for abducting children by luring them with your cooking and food.'

Senga looked carefully at the reflection in the window.

'The people who looked like Chinese on the television, look like North East Indians on the reflection. Don't you think so?'

'What are you arriving at? Are you saying that they are just setting a narrative and that the Chinese story isn't true?'

'Maybe. If they commit to who the enemies are, then they also need to state why they are attacking us. Because you are scared of the reasoning, you guys duck and hide and change the face of your enemies to your convenience! You are part of this sham too!'

'Senga, this is some serious border issue. Not a game!'

'Oh yeah! You always have problems only at the borders. Stay right there! Don't dare to get in.'

'Ok! Let that go. You were talking about some spaceship, right? What is the latest on it?'

'I am bored of making videos on your government's madness. I am sure that the spaceship would also be yet another edition of their madness. So, I left it at that.'

'A sincere government would look whacky through the prism of "normal" eyes!'

'Don't you dare! I shall pour the sugar syrup of the jamun onto your face…. change the topic.'

'Do you like Ludo King?'

'Of course.'

Keerthi and Buvanesh were playing a game of Ludo and Senga and Nithilan joined them. Manjula took her empty casserole and left by shutting the door, quietly behind her.

'Hey Nithi! What is this? She is closing the door as quietly as if she has let us into the room of our nuptial night?'

'Shush! There are kids around.'

'Weren't the kids around when she brought you the gulab jamuns?'

Nithi rolled the dice and got six. He started moving his coin.

Mohan Janarthanan did not have faith in God. But he would visit temples and churches very frequently. He harboured a fond hope that some divine grace would prevail and change his son Machiavelli's mental condition. On that day, when Mohan stepped out of the Santhome Church, Nithilan was waiting for him in the car. They both went up the lighthouse on the Marina shoreline and having reached the top, plonked themselves on chairs. They were served tea. The water on the Bay of Bengal was spread across like a diamond carpet.

'Your demo was very clear this morning. People at the PMO appreciated it.'

'Had you informed me, before the Zoom meeting, that the Prime Minister, Home Minister Rajkumar, Deputy Defence Minister Bahadur Shah, and the Principal Secretary of the Armed Forces Govardhan Sarkar would all be present, I might have made a presentation in greater detail, sir.'

'You might have been tensed and anxious and hence I didn't tell you earlier. They have asked me to make two small changes. Instead of having three different people's thumbprints, they are asking us to incorporate all of it as the Prime Minister's print.'

'Ok...but...'

'But what?'

'Sir, wouldn't it be better to have a three-level security for the box?'

'Nithi, they would make suggestions only after a thousand discussions so we should follow them verbatim. That's our job.'

'Done, sir.'

'After the display of Veer Shivaji's picture, they requested for the sound clip of "Jai Hind".'

'Noted, sir.'

While he observed from that height, Mohan felt that there were two worlds, one belonging to man and the other to nature. He probably found something amusing in it. He had a broad smile on his face, for some private joke or the taste of the tea could have triggered it.

The questions that were running in Nithilan's mind came to rest on his lap. If he were not to pose those questions and keep quiet anymore, he feared that they would jump off the lighthouse and commit suicide.

'Sir, why are we giving so much importance to the catalium roots?'

'Didn't your friend Senga brief about that?'

Nithilan had a sheepish smile and scratched his beard.

'Let her be, sir. She would be blabbering something or the other....'

'You know pretty well that she doesn't blather and I know that too. Some of the young YouTubers today are pretty advanced in their approach. It is astonishing to see the kind of sources that they approach for their news.'

'Sir, is Jelly, a truth?'

'This Jelly is a consequence of the Russia-Ukraine war. A Ukraine-based network company is alleged to have created this Jelly. We do not know the exact truth behind it. Even though Ukraine and the company had asked them to shelve it temporarily, it had leaked out through some resources. Today, every move of ours is decided by data. Just as the geographical strata of the ionosphere, stratosphere, and troposphere, today we are surrounded by datasphere. This Jelly would be on a rampage till it gets the data down to zero state. The Internet is dying. It isn't just that, this Jelly can corrupt all the electronic systems and can make them defunct. Even if no one plans to use the armoury, the weapons stored there would cause some destruction or the other. In some videos, there was even a mention of digital apocalypse and I think that was the most appropriate choice of word.'

'Where does catalium find a place here?'

'When Jelly finishes its game, all the digital assets will be destroyed. The digital world must start all over afresh after the destruction. Everyone would be desperate to retrieve data. They would somehow stumble on a path and set their course. They would then try to restore the network. They would succeed with that too. But no table will have a computer; no one's mobile will work. You cannot rely on the smart grid power source. Digital traffic system will not function!'

'One needs catalium to reset all of it.'

'Exactly. To produce electronic gadgets, they use many metals like Cerium, Germanium, Indium, Selenium, Tantalum, and Tellurium. Research says that catalium roots are a hundred times more effective than all these metals. They have proved that one catalium root ball can produce the inner parts of a few million electronic gadgets. These catalium roots are available only in the Andaman forests. The nature of the soil, the characteristics of the rocks, and the quality of the foliage there bring about this combination, is what they claim. We need to protect them.'

Nithilan sat up straight.

'Sir, how are we going to save them? For how long can we secure them?'

'Isn't that why you have made an invincible locker?'

'It isn't that, sir. Why should we protect the root balls in the box? Can't we let it grow in the forest, in its natural setting? Who can endanger the reserve forests?'

'Did you not see, yesterday, as to what anyone can do? Some terrorists from Nagaland had tried to infiltrate the Andaman forests and tried to poison the roots by using harsh chemicals.

Thank God their attempt was aborted.'

'Was it Nagaland? The news reported them as the Chinese, sir.'

'I did not get to see the news. I am sharing what was reported to me.'

'Why would our own people indulge in this heinous act?'

'They don't consider India as their nation.'

This statement crushed Nithilan's spirits. He was more crumpled than the crushed shirt that Senga gave him.

'And also, Nithi, other countries have sniffed out the fact that we have this magical alternate resource. Do you remember that you had analysed an audio clip, some time back?'

'Yes, sir.'

'There is the threat of the forest area being invaded or destroyed any time soon. So, the PMO is trying to remove as many lakhs of roots as they possibly can from the forest and protect them.'

'Does our job stop with creating the boxes, sir?'

'Do you want to run away after making the boxes? No way!'

Nithilan hid his smile inside the collar of his shirt and dared to spill the last question that he had.

'Where are we going to keep the boxes and protect them, sir?'

Mohan rose. He tied his hands behind him and strolled across while staring at the Bay of Bengal.

Have they built a magical island under the sea? Will we be protecting the boxes under the depths of the sea? Many random ideas were crowding Nithilan's mind. Even before he could voice out his imagination Mohan started laughing.

'Sir, why are you laughing?'

He spilled a part of his laugh before he got around to answering Nithilan.

'Wherever they have planned to secure the catalium root

balls, you and Pramil will have to accompany them.'

'Would be my pleasure, sir.'

'Last week an incident happened. There is no way for you to know about it…'

Nithilan stood up.

'The Home Minister Rajkumar's grandson Sourav, got caught in a riot, but luckily escaped unscathed. Para Commando Nisha Pilot had saved him. The riot had taken place in Vijaypur village, Changlang district, Arunachal Pradesh. Most people who were killed in that riot belonged to the Sangma tribe.'

'Oh!'

'The riot took place in 1994.'

'I don't understand, sir.'

'When do you have a meeting with Nisha Pilot?'

'Wednesday, sir.'

'All the best!'

Pramil did not show half the interest that Nithilan did in the catalium project. 'We have loads of pending work in the Adayal project already; why should we burden ourselves further with this project?' was Pramil's frustration and he was whining about that. Yesterday a large biometric information reached the workstation. One of the data did not have fingerprints. When Pramil enquired, a field volunteer had sent an email claiming that it belonged to a seventy-year-old man and his fingerprints had faded. There were people with fading fingerprints and then there were some who had lost their hands! Problems and issues were lining up in front of Pramil Swaminathan, swamping him and clamouring for his attention. The central committee had assured that in such a case the iris recognition would do.

Auto driver Mahesh had lost his eyes and hands in an accident. How should he be brought under the radar of Adayal was a heated discussion that Pramil took up in the virtual conference that night. Mahesh's daughter Dharini had also made a plea to somehow get her father treated. The conference was concluded on that note.

It was the wedding anniversary of Pramil and Karthika. Pramil had hit the sack at five in the morning after his late-night calls. Karthika did not expect any greeting from him that morning. She was just bidding the right time to hand over the new mobile phone to Pramil—her anniversary gift for him. It was getting late for her. She needed to go to the gym, which she owned. She was not just the boss but she also was an instructor there.

Pramil would hardly converse with Karthika. He barely had any weekends so they never stepped out together to a restaurant or the beach; nor did they go shopping or to the movies. Their only bonding activity in the marriage was to catch up on the movies and web series on the OTT platforms, late at night, in the comfort of their house. Pramil happened to lose interest in sexual intercourse by the time he hit his thirties. Karthika could never revive the interest back for him. After a point of time, she decided that it was not her responsibility and she removed herself from that attempt. Recently she seemed to have a strong inclination to adopt a baby. By the time she was in her forties, the inclination gathered strength.

Karthika wanted to start her seventeenth anniversary with her adopted baby but her wish was not fulfilled. When Pramil opened his eyes that morning, Karthika was standing beside him with a broad smile, her face clean of any expectation.

'Happy anniversary, Pramil!'

'OMG! Hey....Karthi...wish you the same!'

'It's getting late for me. I need to be at the gym. I need to leave. I have left idli and chutney on the table. I have also made a preparation that can be vaguely christened as halwa. Please have your breakfast.'

Pramil had his bath and came to the dining table. He found a greeting card and a gift on the table. He first opened the idli dish. Then munching on the carrot halwa he wondered what the gift could be. Halfway through the unwrapping, he realised that it was a 'OnePlus' mobile phone. Thanks to the high speed of the fan, the greeting card fluttered open and it appeared as if the words spilled out in volition.

Pramil,

We need to talk a lot! Our life and the long days are waiting for us. But a third life is crucial in our life journey. That life is going to add significance and new meaning to the rest of our lives. Please introduce that life to me as soon as possible. I am waiting to see the face of our future.

Happy anniversary greetings!

At work, Nithilan took a good look at the message and smiled broadly.

'What is this, Pramil sir? Have you decided on the face of your future?'

Pramil maintained silence.

'We have booked tickets to New Delhi already. We are leaving on Wednesday, sir.'

'Why don't you go alone Nithi? I have plenty of work to do.'

'Para commando meeting. Prime Minister's Office protocol. I leave it to your discretion, sir.'

Machiavelli was seated in the garden in his backyard and was bawling his eyes off. His right hand had nail scratches. He was trying to hide it from himself. The stink emanating from his school uniform pervaded across the garden. He had picked a hibiscus plant as his companion and was crying next to it. He stared at it unblinkingly. When Mohan Janarthanan entered the house, he didn't search for Mac. He directly went to the garden. He was continuously receiving calls from his organisation and the home ministry office but he ignored them. Mohan sat next to Mac and said nothing but shared Mac's tears companionably. He opened the sweet box that he had bought. It was Mac's favourite chocolate-flavoured *sonpapdi*. Mac picked one from the box and tried to dry his tears. The flakes of *sonpapdi* fell on the nail scratches on his right hand.

Machiavelli was in class six in a special school for mentally challenged kids. His school was gearing up for a science exhibition. The task assigned for class six was to use the sounds of the forest to create a prayer song. They would complete the task with the help of their music teacher. Mac had used the hooting of the owls for his song. It was a musical piece without lyrics. Umar, the class leader, took an exception to Mac's attempt and insisted that the song must be composed as per the instruction and he was hard on Mac.

Machiavelli was sucking into his cocaine lollipop and playing his song and put his head down on the desk and fell fast asleep. Umar came running into the class and gave some tight slaps to the sleeping Mac. Mac woke from his sleep bewildered and the lollipop fell to the floor and broke into pieces. Mac got into a rage and he pushed Umar down. He picked a desk nearby and flung it on Umar. Mac held Umar by his cuff, dragged him near the wall and banged his head on it. Mac clenched his fist and punched hard on Umar's face. He dragged him and pushed him off the stairs. The crowding boys did not interfere for fear of Mac and moved a step back.

Umar screamed in pain and fear. He could not bear the pain. Machiavelli descended the stairs. He sat on the last step where Umar lay flat. In helpless anger, Umar scratched Mac's hands with his nails. Mac lifted Umar by his hands and took him for first aid. While they were attending to Umar, Mac started to wail. He went back to his class, crying all the way. Some of his classmates knocked on his head with their knuckles. Mac went to his seat and collapsed his face onto the desk. 'Where is Machiavelli?' when the teacher came to enquire about him, he was asleep again.

By the time he bit into the second piece of the sweet, Mac's tears had completely dried. Mohan Janarthanan picked up Mac's mobile and started playing his 'owl' music. A sudden darkness fell on the garden and the colours faded. Mac got up and peed on the hibiscus plant.

Ever since Nithilan returned from Delhi, he had been wanting to catch up with Senga. He had a lot to download to her but he somehow could not find the time for it. Penetration testing is a method by which one intrudes into one's own computer and documents and tests its strength of security. He was busy with that test. He wanted to decrypt some information and hence was writing a hashing algorithm for it.

Whatever he was doing, his mind was haunted by 'Veer Jadayu'. It seemed as if Govardhan and Nisha Pilot were standing behind him holding an antique sword to his back. Govardhan spoke a Sanskritised Tamil, while Nisha Pilot spoke a Bangla Tamil and Nithilan felt that he might forget his own unique Tamil because of them.

Senganthal had said that she would be off to ECR for a shoot. She claimed that there was a famous haunted bungalow at Uthandi, ECR; she planned to spend a sleepless night there and interview the ghost that haunted it. Senga's crew had decorated the bungalow with a 'ghostly' atmosphere in honour of the resident ghost! Nithilan joined them.

'What madness is this, Senga? Is there really a ghost here, or are you guys the spirits?'

'Dear, this is just a drama. They are building hype around this Wellington bungalow like the Demonte colony. We wanted to try spending a day and night here and that's why we arrived here with the cameras. All of this is content business. You don't get involved in it.'

'On the one hand, you talk about rational thinking and on the other, you are claiming to interview a ghost?'

Senga was quietly focussing on her makeup.

'Most of your rational-thinking atheist friends seem to be visiting temples, huh?'

'No rational thinker has said that one should not visit temples. Who stopped them?'

'Ah! Then you would take part in festivals for Lord Muruga and go around sporting black shirts, eh?'

'Yes! You are right! Please do not place rational thinking and spirituality on opposite sides. That would be flawed. Rational thinking helps us understand the practicalities of the external world while spirituality throws light on the inner world. Both are different, but both are essential.'

She was using the liner to draw wings to her eyelids. She used it to accentuate her already big bold eyes. It was dusk. The crew was expecting the ghost to appear shortly.

'Senga…'

'Mmhm…what's with this tone?'

'I am worried and scared.'

'Why? About the ghost?'

'I know some truths. You are right next to me. The camera is right across. So, I fear.'

Both of them took a stroll behind the bungalow in the Casuarina grove.

'This is exactly where yesteryear actor Jaishankar would chase the villains, laden with his gun. MGR's movie *Thai Sollai Thattathey* (Follow your mother's words) was filmed right here. The fight sequences were shot here.'

'His name is also Jaishankar.'

'Whose?'

Nithilan leaned on a tree. He could not decide where to start.

'Whatever it is, share it with me, Nithi. I shall not reveal anything to anyone without your permission. I promise this on the next kiss that you are going to give me.'

He gave her that kiss. She bloomed in the victory of her statement.

Nisha Pilot introduced 'Veer Jadayu' to Nithilan in the tunnel workshop in Sanjay Van, Delhi. Nithilan was caught between astonishment over the colossal size of 'Veer Jadayu' and the appreciative curves of Nisha Pilot. He was indeed spoilt for choice! He had presumed 'Veer Jadayu' to be an ordinary train in the shape of a spaceship. But when he grappled with the truth of it, in the information torrent, it seemed like an elephant had stepped into the room!

'Veer Jadayu' was a 'Time Travel Train'! It could go back in time. It had the strength and power to move 20-200 years in the past. It could separate the swirl of time through reverse entropy and change its direction. The technology used for 'Veer Jadayu' had incisive scientific innovation. It functioned on the power of yoga. Just as in the tale of *Alibaba and the Forty Thieves*, where the slaves used a contraption to open the door to the cave, a team of yogis projected their mind waves into the cosmos and connected with the incidences there and made the spaceship function. The purpose and goal of this Time Travel Train was to go to the days and times of mythology and bring back the ideal men to the present, where they were believed to be the figments of imagination.

Pramil, Nithilan, Nisha Pilot, Govardhan, and Jaishankar had travelled in a pocket for a test run. The train took them to the year 1946, to a shooting spot, where a Tamil movie *Chandralekha* was being filmed. The film was popular for its 'drum dance' sequence. Rehearsals were going on for this sequence. Nithilan and Pramil shared a Time second with the heroine of the movie T. R. Rajakumari. Time second was something that would get directly imprinted into the memory tissue. When one revived it through one's memory, it would trigger a similar experience to the person in front like a replay.

Nithilan went into the workshop with plenty of questions hounding his mind. Where would they have safekeeping for the catalium boxes? For how long? But then Nithilan spaced out on all those questions. Nithilan recollected the conversation with Mohan Janarthanan on top of the light house and now realised the shades of 'past' lurking behind Mohan's ghost of a smile.

Just as an infant would listen to the grandma's tales while drinking milk, Senga listened to his narration with wide eyes and avid interest.

'Veer Jadayu?'

'Mmhm.'

'A Time Travel Train that goes to the past?'

'Yes!'

'Won't you ever invent something that takes you forward towards progress?'

Nithilan did not expect that barb.

'You are kidding about everything, right?'

'Absolutely not, Nithi. Your tale is worse than the tale of a ghost in this Wellington Bungalow.'

Nithilan lit a cigarette after many days of abstinence.

'You don't believe what I just said?'

'It's impossible to believe. In 2009, when Stephen Hawking attempted to do time travel, he organised a cocktail party. He clicked a lot of pictures. Only after the party was done, did he advertise the agenda of his experiment. He believed that if time travel was feasible then he thought that someone would read this advertisement from the future and travel back and attend his party. He also believed that such a visitor would also feature in the photographs. He waited all alone, all day long at his party. No such time traveler attended it. Hawking did not condemn that time travel was a lie. But you are claiming that you have succeeded where Hawking failed! That doesn't make sense.'

Nithilan inhaled the cigarette and the smoke that he exhaled hard seemed to move towards ECR.

'The Home Minister's grandson got caught in one of the pockets. It took him to the Vijaypur riots of 1994. Someone had set fire to the refugee camps there. Sourav and Nisha Pilot were caught in the fire and managed to somehow get back to the present alive.'

'1994 is fine. But you are claiming that the train would go to the ancient mythological era, right? That's what scares me. Your people should not drive us back into the thick of the Kurukshetra war of the Mahabharata. I am worried for the people.'

Nithilan tapped on Senga's head, with the fingers in which he held the cigarette.

'Jelly is gradually destroying everybody's living, Nithi. New network errors are cropping. Everywhere the server is down, the machine is corrupt, and the message screams: data not found! App based taxi services are flailing because their software has been washed out; flight services are cancelled. A generation that trusts the Internet for even their essential needs is suffering and going crazy. Our channel shoots are only for banking, not for relay or uploading. We are unable to upload anything. Where is this going to lead us? We do not know! Are you not concerned about all of this? When our present is sinking, what is the point of your farsightedness? People are miserable and you choose time travel as a solution?'

'The government is like a lotus flower. It has a hundred petals. Some will bear the present day and some the future.'

'True that! A lotus would never be attached to the water that gave it sustenance. Similarly, your government is completely indifferent to us, the people, who are responsible for its growth and development.'

'Do you think that we are struggling so hard to protect

an essential thing that our people need for the future without caring for them? Why would we take such a big risk if we are not concerned about the welfare of the people?'

'You say people? You mean you are going to protect that catalium and give it to the people? You would only give it to the corporate bosses. You clamoured digital and digitised everything. Now that there is a big threat to digital data and connectivity, you are not giving people an alternative. Instead, you are boarding a Time Travel Train with catalium. Of what help are you guys?'

Senga's question hit the stars and echoed back.

'One who doesn't have a future would go back to his past, Nithi.'

'Senga, I am neither the ruling party nor a person in power. Why are you killing me with your questions?'

'You are an advisor in their IT wing. Isn't that enough? Even if you are outside, you are still an insider for them.'

'Who else do you think would be the best head in power, for the future, as far as India is concerned?'

'Nithi, you can be loyal to the head or the hair, for all I care! Please do not think that I am dragging you into all the injustice happening around us. You are a bearded toddler, in my opinion! You are not very well versed in things. Our generation is not keen on knowing the details of politics, we shun away and that's our curse! You will also get enraged someday. The questions that I am shooting today will be posed by you tomorrow. I have that belief.'

Nithilan sighed.

'Ok, leave that! Where are you going on that train? Which year?'

'1935. We are going to Seshaiya's mango orchard. Seshaiya was Vallabhbhai Patel's close friend. We are going to store the containers in a cow shed behind the orchard. We would be staying in the guest house in the mango orchard. We will return when they ask us to.'

'Will you meet Vallabhbhai Patel?'

'Certainly! But when I meet him, I shall not ask the questions that you are imposing on me about India.'

Senga's face crumpled. Nithilan patted her cheek.

'Hmm…. you are spinning some kind of yarn. I have to believe you.'

Both of them walked towards the bungalow.

'When we enter the bungalow again, would there be a time travel? Your talk, your fag, and all of it, will it happen again as a rewind?'

Senga pouted her lips and rolled her eyes.

'It would be ok if that happened, Senga. Do you remember the day you gave me a love bite on my back, the hickey you caused? I suppose I don't need to get to the details before that. I can't endure the pain of another bite!'

Senga felt that her personality manifested in Nithilan's cheekiness. Her laughter tinkled like a running brook. She was freshly anxious after entering the bungalow.

'Nithi, should you travel on the 'Veer Jadayu'? Can you not avoid it?'

He expected this question in the casuarina grove itself.

'This is not a technical commitment darling. It is the nation's security. It is my duty to the nation, my national spirit.'

'Your national spirit does not have the strength to save itself! How can it save you? I am scared.'

'It's similar to travelling to Madurai or Kanyakumari. Don't fear.'

Senga leaned on his shoulder. Nithilan found it a trifle difficult to hold her. Senga's weight of anxiety was heavy!

00000000019

Pramil was describing that the true story of the destruction of Kumari Kandam, an ancient Tamil civilisation, was linked to the big tale of Noah's ship, with sufficient proof. Every big civilisation had a story of the deluge and the first one started with Kumari Kandam was his contention. Pramil was very fond of history and he loved keeping the lost pages of history nearby. Mankind was probably found first in Africa, but he firmly believed that civilisation happened first in the lands that are present-day India. He had proved this theory with evidence from palm leaves and stone inscriptions in his blog pages.

'Are we not transporting dogs, cats, birds, and elephants in our Noah? Is it only going to be catalium?'

This was the first question from Nithilan when he met the people arranging for the travel on 'Veer Jadayu'. He had pushed away his plate which contained Good Day biscuits and cashews, as if he didn't like them. He kept si pping water frequently.

'We do not have dogs, cats or birds; but we do have elephants.'

Nithilan presumed that Pramil was referring to catalium as the elephant.

'No! It is not what you are thinking. We are going to distribute 120 crore people's biometric details of Adayal in the 2,000 containers and carry the Adayal data vault with us.'

'You never informed me.'

'The PMO decides who would be told what on a need-to-know basis.'

'Why are we storing them in a distributed manner?

'Why indeed? You tell me. You were the one to give this idea, way back.'

'Ok! Each disc has a key. Only after we connect all the discs, the key will be completed and the data vault will open.'

'Correct!'

Nithilan had yet another doubt.

'Sir, why this circuitous path? It would suffice if we remove the data centre from the network to solve the current problem. Also, we have a backup data centre at a distance of five kilometres from here. How else can we secure the data, sir?'

'It is required, Nithi. We haven't yet received the permission to remove data from the network. We may get it tomorrow. But can we vouch that until now not a single system in our data centre is free of Jelly attack? Do we know for sure whether it has invaded us or not? What if it has? The complete data would be lost. By the time we discover what sort of virus it is, if 120 crore Adayal data gets destroyed, then what? Haven't you noticed that during the riots people mob malls and shops and raid them for gadgets like fridges and TV?—similarly foreign powers are trying to use Jelly as an excuse, and intel that we received says that they are targeting our data centres. We certainly need external backup.'

'Not a joke! Twenty petabyte data! Where will you store it? What storage facility do we have?'

'You have taught us everything and now you are posing questions like a novice!'

Nithilan thought for a few seconds. A grey colour glass disc that he had introduced to his organisation some time back, flashed in his mind.

'Sir, please don't tell me that it is a deep grey glass disc.'

Pramil smiled.

'Sir, it is in its developmental stage. We need to conduct various security testing yet!'

'You have 48 hours to do so.'

'This is a bad joke, sir.'

'We have asked for the Map Port team to join. You will need their help.'

Pramil picked a square glass from his work table. He also showed the camel skin pouch that would protect the glass.

'Sir, we can store only 100 TB of data in this deep grey disc. Adayal data is 20,000 TB. We need 2,000 discs.

'It is ready, Nithi. We have made 2,000 boxes for catalium. Each box will have a layer of catalium at the bottom and a layer of catalium at the top and a glass disc in the middle.'

'You asked for 2,000 boxes, only based on this calculation, is it?'

'Yes.'

'Then isn't catalium important? Is it just a fib? Are we going to have a wolf in sheep's clothing? Are we covering data with catalium?'

'Catalium is important. But our Indian population's complete data is significantly more important. We are using a small relevance to protect the bigger relevance. It is not a wolf in sheep's clothing, it is a wolf cub in wolf's clothing!'

Nithilan scratched his beard.

'Are you confused, Nithi?'

'Yes!'

'That's what the government desires.'

Nithilan sought out the cashews.

'Trying to know everything is like a suicidal attempt. If you want to stay alive and well, it is better to stay confused, not knowing all the details.'

Nithilan found it hard to swallow the bitter truth that Pramil had shoved down his throat, compelling him to wash it down with a glass of water.

Irrelevant details are removed in the process of iris recognition. Data related to its circumference, colour, and lines are gathered in the data archive squares. The three sizes are changed into a number, and numerical calculations are made by the computer. An individual's data on his iris is registered as a unique negative number. These registrations are sent to the central computers. In this iris centre not, many people have entry access; Nithilan didn't have access. If they had to do a test run for security reasons, they needed to get prior approval from the ministry. Or Pramil had to raise a request and Mohan Janarthanan must treat it as urgent and give special permission.

'We need to take the backup of iris data, sir. Server machines and cloud operations are all getting corrupt.'

Kamalesh Yadav, who was working at the iris centre had raised a request to Pramil Swaminathan. Mohan Janarthanan was offering to make copies of the data for Pramil when Nithilan entered the room with a box. He had changed the configuration such that the boxes would open only with the Prime Minister's fingerprints. He had rewritten the programs so that the sound clip of Jai Hind appeared once Veer Shivaji's image was displayed.

On the terrace of his multi-storeyed apartment, parrots visited at 5 p.m., pigeons at 5:30 p.m. and crows at 6 p.m.

Nithilan came up to the terrace late that evening around 7 p.m. By then the birds were done with their visit. He was trying to find their feathers as a mark that they had left behind, after their customary visit. He was desperately searching for their traces. He felt that if Senga were around, he could find some of the traces at least. He noticed the usual traffic snarl on the roads. A small crowd was thronging around the masala vada shop. A young woman who was trying to take a selfie with the vada lost her balance and dropped the vada. Her friends raised a ruckus for that. Digital apocalypse, my foot! Our people have learned to live around whatever happened to them—the fallen vada was spouting this philosophy until a stray dog came and picked it up.

Aagol | 87

'Why do you wear this dirty shirt without washing?'
'Why? What's wrong with this shirt?'
'If you are a security, you must wear a firmly starched and ironed shirt, right?'
'Who is there for me to starch my shirt?'
'Don't you have a wife?'
'She eloped with someone.'

The maid who came to the third floor felt that she had nothing more to pursue than a conversation with the security. She had expressed her regret to the old man, who was the security of the apartment through her pointed conversation and now that she was done, she pedalled away on her cycle. His shirt had always been dirty, but it took a maid to observe and ask that question. Why is it that no resident of the apartment ever asked him or thought of asking him that question? Nithilan, who was observing this interaction from his top floor, felt that his question died as it sprang to life.

Government staff were working on a war footing all across the country to relay the old cables of telecommunication and were also laying new ones underground. These works were happening in his street too. The view from the terrace made him imagine the open trenches dug by the employees to be the irises of the eyes gaping back at him! They were getting some excuse or the other to dig up the roads and let them be.

There were about 10 to 12 caged pigeons in the tunnel workshop at Sanjay Van. Maybe the prime minister would free these pigeons as a mark of peace before he flagged off 'Veer Jadayu'? 'Would they have a mega shooting with the prime minister and the pigeons?' The employees who were loading the catalium boxes in one of the pockets were muttering to themselves. Nithilan had arrived at Delhi but was hesitant to board the time train. In case he didn't return alive, what would happen to the dreams he had woven about his life with Senganthal? Nithilan could not focus on Linga's lecture on the functionalities of 'Veer Jadayu'.

Nithilan did not believe when Linga asked them to use the wing wave technology to connect the people in the past and present when they travelled. The researchers had found that one could move beyond the neutrino wave zone but had not mentioned that one could travel beyond time. Linga was a member of the South Asian Electrical Wave Research Circle and hence he could debate on all the learnings about neutrinos.

Neutrino was ready to get in touch and connect with the past. But to move it beyond time 'a propulsive wave' was required; this was the discussion that the scientists had with Linga. Linga had created that propulsion from the flapping of the wings of the birds. But it had to be the first flap of wings when the bird was about to launch into a flight from the ground or a branch. Linga had discovered equipment that would convert the ecstatic delight of that moment into a propulsive wave. With this propulsion, the neutrino waves would create a connection with the past through a contraption that was light yellow. It looked like a crab with a topknot and Linga called it 'Atharvana'. He was given that name by the high command.

Jaishankar and Nisha Pilot wanted to test the communication

system of 'Atharvana'. So, they stepped into a pocket of 'Veer Jadayu' and went to the year 1996 to Chennai. They arrived at Kalaignar Karunanidhi's campaign meeting. Jaishankar carried an 'Atharvana' with him. The pigeon cage in Sanjay Van was opened. Linga asked them to open the windows in the workshop. The principal secretary of the armed forces, Govardhan himself walked up to the windows and opened them. Linga claimed that when the birds started flying towards the skies, he would get the propulsion needed to activate his device. When the birds started flapping their wings and were about to take off to the skies, he kept his 'Atharvana' device right next to them and switched it on. The engineers sitting in a corner of the workshop jumped to action on the command console of 'Atharvana,' stationed in their corner.

Jaishankar was standing behind the stage in the campaign meet and was carrying 'Atharvana' in his hand. It created a sound that seemed as if five Sanskrit words were strung together and spewed out. He pressed the button. Linga handed over the device to Govardhan.

'Calling from the land of Bharat.'

Nisha Pilot smiled when she heard Govardhan's voice.

'Call received. Your voice is crystal clear. Jai Hind.'

As Nisha responded they could hear Karunanidhi's voice from the stage too. It took Pramil some seconds to absorb that voice which came through time travel to his ears.

'You call us.'

Linga disconnected.

Jaishankar spotted some birds in a park next to the stage. He rushed near the birds, made them flutter away and held 'Atharvana' next to them. He did not get the connection. Everyone on the other side was waiting in eager anticipation.

A bird was seated on the swing in the park. Nisha Pilot took 'Atharvana' from Jaishankar and approached the swing stealthily.

She waited for the bird to take off. When it did, she held the device right next to it. She was connected.

'Nisha Pilot, reporting from 1996.'

'Well done, Linga,' Govardhan clapped in approval. The employees and staff in the workshop followed him with thunderous applause.

'Won't the device work if the birds fly as a flock?'

Jaishankar wanted to know the reason why he failed to connect in his attempt.

'No! There are just two conditions. First, it should be the bird's first flap of wings at that time. Second, the bird must fly at its own will. You need to wait until then. Only then we shall get that ecstatic delight we need for the propulsion. If the bird flies in fear, because it was startled by someone, then we will not get the connectivity.'

Nisha Pilot grinned at Jaishankar. They disconnected. Both of them returned to the present time.

Linga said that he was trying to get the neutrino connectivity to Govardhan's and Pramil's laptops. Nithilan wondered if he would get one too.

That evening, Govardhan, Nisha Pilot, Jaishankar, Pramil, and about twenty employees were reading the conditions to fly in 'Veer Jadayu,' quite intently.

Every pocket of the time train had five-star facilities built into it. Govardhan's pocket had an additional facility—a swimming pool.

Nithilan was caught in an inexplicable panic. To come out of it, he started playing his favourite Tamil song, which went something like, 'Golden girl, a golden doll like you…...' It played like an anthem praising the 'Veer Jadayu's' mission. The staff clapped along with the beat. Nithilan hoped that their palms would not get stuck together and smiled to himself!

Machiavelli did not know how to spend a night without power. There was a huge power outage!

Mohan Janarthanan did not make any attempt to go to the motor room to fetch diesel and fill the inverter to restore the temporary power connection. He accepted darkness as it was.

Sirrius storage had received many iris recognition data from the various districts of Rajasthan that day. Mohan was checking the first committee's report to see if there was any false data. Mohan believed that a man's story was piled on his eyes. Every iris data that he opened seemed to narrate a tale of its own. It scared him as it was midnight so he shut his laptop down.

Machiavelli was huddled in the corner of the room like a white cat. He was playing piano on his mobile. As he kept playing the piano, the charge in the mobile was getting drained. At one point the music came to a halt. The feeble light in that room was also switched off then.

'Shall we play pitch-dark cricket?'

When Mohan asked this question, he immediately agreed.

Mohan shut the curtains of the window so that the room became darker and they could not see shape, form, object, or shadow. Father and son started playing cricket. They could not see the person standing opposite to them. They could not see the ball, the bowling, or the bat. The bowler must bowl the ball towards the batsman perceptively. When the ball rolled on the ground the batsman must hear the sound of the ball and hit it. The bowler in his turn must field the ball hearing the sound and bowl again.

Mohan did not even expect Machiavelli to hit every ball with precision. It was difficult for Mohan to hear the sound of the ball and predict its direction. He got used to it in ten minutes though. Machiavelli played much better in the dark than in broad daylight.

It was the first ball of the sixth over. When Mohan bowled, he noticed that Machiavelli did not hit it. He picked the ball and bowled again. He couldn't hear any sound of the ball being hit. He called out, 'Maci, Machiavelli...!' but did not receive any response. Mohan took out his mobile from his pocket and switched it on for some light. Machiavelli was not in the room. He checked out the whole house with his mobile light.

Machiavelli was missing.

00000000022

Lokabhiramam ranarangadhiram
Rajivanetram raghuvanshanatham
Karunyarupam karunakaram tam
Shri ramachandram sharanam prapadye
Nilambujashyamalakomalangam
Sitasamaropitavamabhagam
Panau mahasayaka charu chapam
Namami ramam raghuvanshanatham
Maha Rathna Peete Shubhe Kalpa Moole,
Shukaseenamadhitya Koti Prakasam,
Sada Janaki Lakshmanopethamekam,
Sada Ramachandram Bhajeham, Bhajeham.

'Veer Jadayu' started after this prayer. The yogis who would run this time train were in the centre of the train, wearing their ascetic clothes. Nithilan, Pramil, and Nisha Pilot were traveling in the pocket next to that. Govardhan was assigned a separate pocket. He was poring over the 1930s Indian map. The staff did not have individual pockets. They stayed in the rooms where the catalium boxes were arranged. The 2,000 boxes that contained India's future were moving towards the past.

Nisha was draped in a sari. Along with her para commando role, she was also asked to greet Vallabhbhai Patel with the ceremonial *aarti*. She was wearing her armour inside the sari. Her guns and knives were snuck under her armour. When she sat down, she seemed like a shawled armoury, a covered battlefield!

'Madam, you look good in a sari!'

Pramil broke the silence in the pocket.

Nisha Pilot graced him with a smile of pride. The smile had

a unique colour which was not found in her multicoloured sari.

Had he known that Nisha would appreciate Pramil's praise, Nithilan would have jumped in first with the compliment. He regretted that he didn't offer first.

'Nithilan, why did you shave? Your beard was making you look manly.'

Nithilan did not expect this bouncer from Nisha.

'No issues madam! It can be grown in the snap of a finger.'

Nisha Pilot burst into a sudden laughter as if a bullet had been shot!

'There's a reason ma'am. He shaved the beard off because he is going to be separated from his girlfriend.'

Pramil wanted to establish that Nithilan was not single.

'Interesting, Nithi. You have a beard when she is around, and have a clean-shaven look when separated. You seem to be travelling in reverse.'

'Ma'am, are we all not travelling in reverse now?'

'Don't ma'am me! Call me Nisha.'

For a second confusion prevailed for they did not know, to whom she addressed this message.

'I am telling both of you.'

She tore into the confusion herself and shredded it.

'Ma'am, sorry Nisha, how come you speak such good Tamil?'

'My mom is a Bengali, dad is from Tanjore. Even otherwise, when we go for commando operations, we gain proficiency in the language of that place. Language is also a way of self-defence. Language training is also a weapon training for us.'

'Nisha, I have a doubt. I asked Nithi. He also is not sure of it. You tell me. Is this train running on the technology of reverse entropy created by Jaishankar and his team of engineers, or on the mantras chanted by the yogis?'

'I think both complement each other. We have not been

trained in this Jadayu technology. So, I am not sure if I can answer your questions correctly. But I know one thing for sure. This train is not running because of the mantras chanted by the yogis, but only powered by their thoughts. Mantras are a medium for their thoughts. This train is not running on our ground. It is running on an under-universe hyperbolic track. Thoughts have all sorts of power. If one knows how to handle them, thoughts traverse boundaries. Our old religion teaches us how to handle the power of our thoughts.'

'It looks like you have done your para commando training elsewhere!'

Nisha was not pleased with Pramil's words and insinuation. She felt that if she chatted any further with them, she might lose her respect and moved away quietly.

'What you say is true, Nisha. But Pramil sir does not believe in all this. Only Jaishankar might be able to give him a satisfactory reply.'

Nithilan tried to patch up that small friction. It didn't seem to work or do the needful and so he turned his gaze towards the window.

The train seemed to be passing through various times of years. The grounds and space seemed to be constantly changing. People, their appearances, and clothes were also changing. The gap between one person and the other was expanding. The distance between people and animals was reducing. There was a different tone to the sound of rain. Quite often there was blood splatter on the window. Children who were breathless because of poisonous gases came running along for a short distance. Bent-down heads sometimes flung themselves across the windows, crashed, and fell. Torn saris flew across and tried to rest some time on the windows. People burning alive banged on the windows and collapsed. Times changed but the skies and violence trailed along.

Chief Engineer Jaishankar was seated in the control and command room and monitored the train's speed and the geographical terrain that it was crossing. Four other deputy engineers were working along with him. One of them was converting the yogis' thoughts into directions and fuel with the help of mechanical whips. The screen that researched the drift of thoughts displayed them as serrated lines. Jaishankar was checking on it very often. He was caught in a deep thought about how to tackle a collision, in case another time train crossed their path when they were getting into the past. But he didn't share his worry with anyone. Actor Jaishankar would act in movies where he would investigate intriguing mysteries as a CID officer. He would hold his anxious thoughts to himself and show a pleasant and calm demeanour to the heroine. Jaishankar, the chief engineer, was in the same state of alertness and intensity but schooled a calm face.

The train crossed 1947. Every pocket displayed the year on the notice screen.

'We have crossed India, within India.'

This golden sentence fell on Nithilan and Nisha's deaf ears. The train moved faster than usual and gave them a sense of discomfort.

Nisha Pilot stood up urgently and rushed to the control room. She realised that Jadayu was racing past its stipulated speed by looking at the anxious faces of the engineers.

'Jaishankar sir, what is the issue?'

'It's a time variable bug. We will set it right soon.'

'Should I do anything about it?'

'Please stay calm in your assigned pockets. That would do. Your panic should not affect our yogic pattern. Stay calm.'

Nisha Pilot went to Govardhan's pocket, had a few words with him, and returned to her pocket. The staff were running around in fear. 'Veer Jadayu's' pace kept increasing.

The train had gone past its destination year of 1935.

'What the hell!'

Nisha Pilot rushed back to the control room. Nithilan accompanied her with his half-eaten Subway sandwich. Govardhan was having a heated discussion with Jaishankar. When Nithilan and Nisha opened the door of the room, the train lost its balance. 'Omg! Help! Save! Mom!' all the inmates of the train screamed for help. Panic set in. Some of the staff fainted in fright.

Nithilan rushed to save Pramil. He was crushed under the seat. He carried him on his shoulder and stepped out of the pocket when 'Veer Jadayu' came to a grinding halt with the explosive noise of an earthquake. Pramil rolled off the shoulder.

Nisha Pilot was half conscious on the floor. She held herself up by pressing her hands to the floor, slowly gripped the rails on the pathway of the train rose and looked out of the broken window. An old night was waiting intactly for them.

It wasn't even two months since Chinna Mayan had started wearing dhoti. The dhoti wouldn't stay in his waist even for two minutes. Though he was eight years old, he had a baby face. He looked barely five. He had long hair and he had made an intricate topknot and held it together with a stick from the palm tree. He was wearing a big ear stud that made a cheerful noise when he moved his head. He was so frail and thin that even a fox stuck in a famine might not consider him a good meal. It was way past midnight and the place was desolate. He was holding a tiffin box by its handle and screwing it in his left hand; he jumped onto the sugar cane plantation's narrow path from the Kaliyamman ridge. He was holding a lantern on his right and its glass dome was scraping on his dhoti.

Watchman Aanguthevan had made a makeshift bed with coconut palm leaves while staying on watch. He was seated on it. As soon as he spotted Chinna Mayan, he removed his turban and stood up in respect, clutching onto the ebony staff.

'Welcome dear.'

Chinna Mayan handed over the tiffin box. Aangu received it with respect. Though the person who brought him food was his boss's son, Aangu did not have fear or respect but a servile affection.

Aangu's family had been guarding, Chinna Mayan's father Cheeni Thevan's fields for many generations now.

Aangu's dad Aanachathan was arrested by the Madurai police and was sent into exile to Penang Islands. Aangu had to take over the responsibility of taking care of his family and work for a living. Aangu was travelling in the train which was going from Burma to Madurai. It was laden with sacks of grains. Aangu was taking the train to travel elsewhere to plan a robbery. But when he heard of his dad's fate he decided to come back to his family and took up the position of the guard of the fields.

Aangu was a sturdy man with broad shoulders. He could easily carry fifteen kids like Chinna Mayan on his shoulder and hide inside the sugar cane plantation. He single-handedly chased three wild buffaloes that entered and attacked the village. They called him the 'Buffalo Chaser' Aanguthevan. As days went by, only his tag, Buffalo Chaser, remained. Chinna Mayan shortened that too!

'Buffalo brother, mother has sent pearl millet rice and onions.'

Aangu scratched his head.

'Did you want your wages to be increased? Father said he would keep it in account and give it to you at the time of sugarcane harvest.'

'Ok, son.'

A hedgehog jumped and ran into Chinna Mayan's dhoti. He was terrified and removed his dhoti and shook it well. Aangu was about to crush it with his staff. It was jumping around.

'Wait here, dear. Let me bring a sharp hook to hunt the hedgehog.'

Chinna Mayan stopped him.

Now the hedgehog jumped onto Aangu's dhoti. Chinna Mayan bent down scooped some mud and threw it on the hedgehog. It curled up.

'This would not harm us, buffalo brother! It would just be. If we throw some mud on it, it would curl up. If need be, we can gather it up and eat it. It is good for cough.'

Chinna Mayan picked up the hedgehog and gave it to Aangu. Aangu received it with great devotion like a temple offering.

'Who briefed you with all these details, son?'

'My sister did. In the night, before I go to sleep my elder

sister would tell me a lot of stories about the adventures that my dad encountered in the fields and forests.'

'Very good, dear son. You shouldn't stay in the wild anymore. Pigs and ghosts will be wandering around. So please go home.'

'I shall watch the house and you watch the fields.'

'We shall do just that, my son.'

Not knowing how to handle the dhoti, he picked it up and tied it to his chest. Chinna Mayan picked up the lantern and walked towards the Big House in Perumanallur.

24

'Does Mandayan need this? Why does he do all of this? He should contain himself to guarding the funeral grounds and doing the rituals.'

Karuvayan was grumbling under the tamarind tree. Koniyan alias Kottavi, who was the panchayat office's sweeper, was sitting right next to him, without having any strength to listen to his constant griping.

'What has gone wrong now? Why are you chiding him?'

'You ask me what is wrong? Last month he had brought a stranger to the *choultry* (a resting place). He claimed that the fraud was a wheat merchant from the north. That fraud stole a hundred sacks of paddy from the Big House!'

'But our Buffalo Chaser seized him and made him stand in the centre of the village, right?'

'Mandayan, that useless fellow, has now brought a gang from abroad and made them stay in the choultry.'

'Who are they?'

Kottavi, who was scratching his arse, questioned him with disinterest.

'The place where you are scratching isn't good!'

The question was still plastered on Kottavi's face.

'Mandayan gave some details. I didn't understand anything. The visitors had lost their way and were lying in the Usilampatti funeral grounds like the pyre, wooden and seemingly lifeless. They were about to be attacked and killed by the foxes. Mandayan saved them and brought them into the village. Had I been there I would have chased them back to the foreign lands.'

'Had you gone, they would have chosen the foxes over you and would have made huts in the middle of the forest.'

Karuvayan was quite aware of Kottavi's caustic nature and also knew that he had a stinging tongue, which he unleashed at the most unexpected moment. He could feel the sharp sting of this comment.

'Hey Karuvaya, I heard that amidst the funeral pyre is a fair creature, huh?'

Kottavi unravelled the only information that he had and winked at Karuvayan.

'I must have been careful and realised your leery thoughts when you started scratching. Move away! I am carrying food for them.'

'Hey! If given a chance you might feed them milk with a conch and bury them under, huh?!'

Karuvayan's bullock cart had two big urns; one filled with rice and another with meat gravy. A small pot was brimming with guavas and bananas. Plantain leaves were bundled up. Kottavi gaped at the delicacies.

'You seem to be using the opportunity for visitors to have festive food.'

'Are you crazy? Society people asked me to take it for them and I obliged. I have plenty of chores to do at Vandipettai. Bye!'

When Karuvayan's bullock cart crossed him, Kottavi tried to fill his lungs with the aroma of cooked meat and guavas, one last time.

Nithilan and Nisha somehow manoeuvered to open the door and step out of the derailed time train. They could figure out that they were not in the present time, but beyond that they were clueless. Jaishankar stepped out and was accompanied by Govardhan. The yogis were unconscious in their pockets. The staff recovered from their various bruises and grazes, and awaited Govardhan and Nisha Pilot's next set of instructions.

They could see a rock building at a distance. Nithilan took out his mobile phone. Its torch light sent long rays of light. He observed that many corpses were buried there. Mounds were visible. They had to land in a mango orchard but instead, they landed in a cemetery.

For a long time, Jaishankar and his deputies, who were fiddling around 'Veer Jadayu's' electronic drivers and time plates, suddenly raised their thumbs at Govardhan who was smoking at some distance. The train was ready to start. But 'Veer Jadayu' could go back only to the present world. It could not stop in the year 1935 or midway. Its current design had this constraint.

'We don't have a choice. We should return to our current world.'

Nithilan nodded his head in agreement with what Nisha Pilot suggested. But Govardhan had a different idea.

'If we go back again, are you suggesting that we start all over, Nisha? Should the government cough up a fresh budget? It has taken ₹427 crores for us to reach here. If we return without accomplishing the mission, we have to refund the money. Can you afford it?'

As Nithilan, the Chief Engineer Jaishankar, and many staff belonged to Tamil Nadu, Govardhan was determined to converse in Tamil, throughout the journey. The money that he mentioned in front of all of them froze everyone and they all looked as if they were in the coffins already!

One of the staff members came running to them from a distance.

'Sir, we have landed in Usilampatti burial ground. It is written there on the nameplate.'

Govardhan caught Jaishankar's eye. Jaishankar started adding further details as if he was keyed to reveal the information.

'On calculating the speed and time with which Jadayu moved from the year 1935, we are now in the year 1919–1920. This is British India's Chennai province.'

'Have the container boxes faced any damage?'

Nisha zoned into Govardhan's one-point agenda.

'Five boxes alone have some external scratches. There is no possibility of any internal damages.'

Nithilan reported his inspection efficiently in two sentences.

Govardhan, who was dressed in his army finery, walked into the burial ground toting his cigarette. He twirled his canon-like luxuriant moustache. The corpses murmured that he was a modern *Sudalai Madan* (Believed to be a cremation ground's God). He returned after he had completed smoking his cigarette.

Govardhan asked them to bury the 2,000 boxes in the burial ground, just as Nisha Pilot expected. Nithilan was about to protest but Nisha stopped him just in time.

The staff got on the job half-heartedly. Nisha Pilot removed her sari, got going with her commando dress and picked a shovel to help. Nithilan lent a helping hand. He could not withstand it for long.

After burying the boxes, they placed long sticks randomly. They tied circular plates which had the symbol of Ashoka Chakra etched on them. They collected the jasmine flowers and lemons strewed around and decorated the plates and sticks. They created symbols to identify the place where the boxes were buried. Nithilan tied a small ant-sized mini-tracker device. They could monitor the boxes through this tracker device from a distance of ten kilometres. If there were any suspicious movements, Nithilan's watch would raise an alarm and warn them.

'The yogis are unconscious. How will the train run without their efforts and cooperation?'

'These yogis can help us only to go retro—into the past. To go forward, the scientific gadgets of 'Veer Jadayu' would suffice,' Jaishankar shared this truth with them.

After seeing off Jaishankar and the staff in the Time Travel Train, Pramil, Nithilan, Govardhan, and Nisha entered the burial ground carrying their belongings; in the blink of an eye a pack of foxes surrounded them. Nithilan hid behind Pramil in his panic. Pramil was already trying to hide behind Nisha Pilot. Govardhan lit his second cigarette without any undue drama.

'Has the big guy decided to die after a last smoke?'

Pramil whispered into Nithilan's ears.

When the foxes approached them closer, they could see the desire for meat frothing in the foxes' faces. Nithilan contemplated breaking the circle and running away on his own. Nisha Pilot aimed her gun at an old fox. Govardhan gestured her to pause.

'Should we just die here?'

Nithilan had a spine-chilling moment.

Just then a slender figure came running towards them as if the darkness of the skies piled on them! He had a stout stick in his hand.

'Who is it? So late in the night?'

The foxes were not waiting for the introductions to be made and started moving closer. They moved forward and came into the inner circle and the stranger stepped right in the middle. With not a second to spare, he twirled his stick sharply and quickly. Two foxes that were caught in the twirl were flung far away into the thorny shrubs. He howled at them with a loud noise and kept twirling and hurting them. He chased the foxes away.

'*Thambi* (a term of endearment for younger men), what is your name?'

Govardhan had completely moved from Delhi to Usilampatti. The proof was in him calling the man affectionately in Tamil as Thambi!

'Mandayan, Aiya! (a term of respect) I guard this burial ground. Who are you?'

Govardhan's tale of introduction should be their passport, which would let them stay in this village for the next few days. Pramil, Nithilan, and Nisha were eagerly waiting to hear what he would say. Just then one of the foxes that had fallen on the thorny shrub was getting geared to pounce on Govardhan. He threw the burning cigarette on it. When it still came forward near his feet, he used his boots to crush its head. It spewed blood and died. Nithilan felt that his neck had been crushed and became breathless. Mandayan grinned with his full teeth exposed; they were stained.

'You look like an important man. From which place are you coming, Aiya?'

Govardhan had planned his tale in the time that he had used to kill the fox. Having gathered his thoughts he said, 'We have come from foreign lands to research the environment. I am Professor Govardhan. These three people are my students.'

Mandayan nodded his head vigorously as if he understood every word that he heard.

'I think you are involved in some brainy work. Does this burial ground have the environment that you are researching?'

'No Mr. Mandayan. We have lost our way. Is there any place

nearby where we can stay? Do you have a panchayat hall or….?'

When Nisha Pilot stammered for the right word, Nithilan helped her by providing the word, choultry.

'Choultry? Yes, I will take you. Walk with me.'

Govardhan gestured to the rest, warning them about not revealing too much or talking to Mandayan unnecessarily. Pramil was constantly overstepping such instructions.

'Will we get some tea, nearby?'

Mandayan grinned broadly.

'Which newspaper comes to this village in the mornings?'

Mandayan walked faster.

'Does your choultry have an Indian toilet or a Western toilet?'

Nithilan lost his patience.

'Pramil sir, in our modern India itself we have not completed building toilets in all places. What is the point in asking here? Please come quietly.'

Pramil would not stop.

'Will you be able to twirl this one stick and ward off all the foxes that come to attack?'

'Aiya! It is our smarts that decide whether we are caught by the foxes or the foxes are caught by us. Aiya stamped so forcibly… what a display of strength! The crushing bone would have spelled fear for foxes in ten other villages and they must have ended up in diarrhoea.'

Pramil looked at Govardhan, who was staring at him as if to say that the next stamping of the boots would be Pramil's neck.

They crossed the Kaliyamman ridge, Karuppu temple under the banyan tree, and in the last fading rays of moonlight, they reached the Perumanallur choultry.

Their first day was spent searching for a bird. They had to use 'Atharvana' and connect to their current world and speak to Home Secretary Linga and only then proceed to the next step. It was Govardhan's express order.

Right across the choultry was a house. They had covered a basket and made a makeshift coop for their hens. One of the hens had escaped from under the basket and was running around. Nithilan and Nisha chased the hen. It was constantly running about and seemed to have no intention of flying. Linga had already warned them that the bird must fly on its own and should not be taking a fright-flight. It didn't seem like the hen would fly on its own.

The village kids thought that Nisha and Nithilan wanted to catch the hen and so joined the fray. One of them was so adept that he made one pounce and caught the hen and handed it over as a trophy to Nithilan.

'Here brother, please have it. Make a gravy and eat.'

The four walked a distance from where they were staying and moved into a rugged terrain on the outskirts of the village. They waited behind a crow for some time and when it started flying, they operated 'Atharvana'.

The people in the connectivity room in Sanjay Van got cheerful. They had been waiting for this call eagerly for a long time. Linga was seated outside the workshop and signing some government files. When he heard about the call, he rushed to the connection room.

'Govardhan from Perumanallur, 1920.'

'Linga from Bharat, 2032.'

'Everything is under control!'

'Great, sir. I wanted to give you an alert.'

'What is it?'

'You are in the area of criminal tribes. There is going to be a riot there in the next month.'

'What should we do?'

'Please don't get involved in anything. Do not leave any mark of yours in that year. Stay away from the people there.'

'For how long, Linga?'

'Only for a few days, sir. Pramil, Nithilan…?'

'Sir, right here.'

'We have some bad news. The whole of the Adayal data centre has gone corrupt. Not sure as to how long the backup data centre would be live and functional.'

'Sir, all the backup data is safe here.'

'It should be. It must be! Not a single box should go missing. They must stay safe. Is Nisha around?'

'Speaking, sir.'

'Do you have weapons?'

'Yes, sir.'

'Do not use any of them. A single act of yours there will impact and affect many here. If you shoot a person there, a hundred of them will be affected here. Beware!'

'Done, sir.'

'Govardhan sir, your wife is anxious to know if you have carried your diabetic pills.'

'All good, Linga.'

'Stay safe, sir. Take care!'

Nithilan expected that they would send an alternate train and ask them to go to the mango orchard. He paused for a moment and wondered what would Senganthal have enquired like Govardhan's wife asking about medicines. He was standing on the ridge in that rugged terrain and was caught up in his imaginary world. A stone came flying from nowhere and grazed his earlobe.

On the plains, children were playing a game of pelting stones. They were tying coloured ribbons in their hands.

'Where did you get these ribbons, boys? They look good.' Pramil enquired.

'Ravuthar gave it at the marketplace.'

'Where is the marketplace?'

'There, west of the tamarind tree.'

Merchants belonging to Perumanallur, Kalappanpatti, Murugampatti, and Usilampatti displayed their wares once a month in a common marketplace and it had a festive look. The farmers and merchants from other towns and villages also participated in it after obtaining permission from the local panchayat.

Govardhan returned to the choultry. Pramil, Nisha, and Nithilan went to take a look at the marketplace. The place where they were negotiating prices for the goats had become a ruckus as the negotiation ended up as a heated clash. They ignored that and visited Pazhaniyamma's stall. She was selling dried fish and the smell and crowd jostling them was so strong that they staggered out.

'They have come from abroad and are checking on twirling of sticks.'

Virumayakkal was selling buttermilk. A crowd that had gathered there was discussing the three new visitors. Govardhan's environment story had been interpreted as twirling the stick. Nithilan clarified to Nisha that it may go through many more changes and interpretations.

Chinna Mayan was retying the dhoti as tightly as he could for it slipped very often. He was nagging his elder sister to buy *jeerani* (a special sweet made near Madurai, like a jalebi) from the confectionery store. She ignored him, patted his head and dragged him to the gypsy shop. There were different kinds of combs stacked there. She bought a comb made of a bullhorn and hid it safely in her sari. Later, she went to check out the clothes in the Ravuthar store. Chinna Mayan shrugged her off and sat near the butchers. Huge strips of goat meat were being cut and sold.

An elderly man bought meat, stored it in a coir basket and moved on. He tripped over the huge coil of rope that was used for pegging the tents and fell. Nithilan rushed to help him. Virumayakkal also came to help the person. Nithilan collected the meat pieces and put them back in the basket. The old man gave a chunk of meat to Nithilan in gratitude. He also gave him a dried palm leaf to pack the meat.

'What are you going to do with raw meat? Give it to someone.'

Pramil walked towards the vegetable shops.

Nithilan wondered as to whom he should give it to. He noticed a young boy seated outside the shop. He was crying out loud. He approached the boy and gave him the meat wrapped in the palm leaf.

'Jeerani?'

Nithilan did not understand.

'This is not jeerani, it is goat meat.'

'I want jeerani.'

'Who are you? Why are you alone here? What is your name?'

'Why do you need a name? Get jeerani.'

Nithilan decided that his name must be more valuable than jeerani. Nithilan did not have the local currency to buy anything. He only had the currency of independent India. What could he purchase with that currency in an India that was suffering slavery? Will they accept?

'Ok, come, let's go.'

He took Chinna Mayan to the confectionery store. He

handed over the ten-rupee note that he had.

'What is this, Aiya? Is it a foreign currency?'

'Yes. If you convert it to your currency, you can buy your whole shop for its worth. Please keep this and give jeerani to this child.'

'You keep your money, Aiya. Why do I need money to give sweets to Chinna Mayan? Come here, son. Take to your heart's content.'

Chinna Mayan wiped his eyes and put his hands inside the brass vessel where jeerani were stacked and picked as many as he could. A few pieces broke and scattered down. Nithilan bent down and picked them up.

'It's ok, uncle. You keep them.'

Chinna Mayan sounded generous. Nithilan did not expect that charity. He held the boy's hand and walked back to the meat shop.

'Is your name Chinna Mayan?'

'Sadayathevan Chinna Mayan.'

'My name is Nithilan.'

'*Nethili*…like the fish?'

'Ni-thi-la-n'

He broke a jeerani piece and started munching.

'With whom did you come?'

'There…'

His elder sister was stepping out of Ravuthar store and was searching for her brother. Chinna Mayan freed his hands from Nithilan, ran to his sister, and held her hands. His eyes alone were focussed on Nithilan.

'Where did you get lost? What is all this?'

'Uncle.'

He pointed a finger at Nithilan. She looked up and caught Nithilan's eyes and then walked hurriedly. Nithilan was relishing the jeerani given by Chinna Mayan and he was joined by Pramil and Nisha. The three walked towards the choultry.

Karuvayan's bullock cart was awaiting them at the choultry's entrance.

Inspector Nagamalai was seated in the verandah of the Sindhupatti police station. Madurai collector's office had given him two new registers: Perumanallur 10-1-A and 10-1-B. He was using a pencil to draw lines in them. There was a glass of black coffee next to him.

Kandan of Perumanallur was locked up in the jail. He was arrested the previous night on the charge of stealing a goat from the house of Melatheru Murugampatti's landlord and locked up. Though they caught Kandan, there was no trace of the goat that he had allegedly stolen.

Madurai police station had instructed the cattle owners to make a stamp of their seals on the faces of the animals so that they would be easy to identify when they go missing or get stolen. As per that instruction, the landlord's goat had the seal of a *vel* (javelin). But no such goat was found in the village.

'If the goat had been cooked as a biryani, what's with the seal or javelin?'

Inspector Nagamalai was frustrated.

A complaint was lodged against Kandan who was a driver at the landlord's house. When Kandan heard that there was a complaint lodged against him, he came to the police station personally to sort it out. They arrested him and sent word to the landlord. Coming to the police station or being jailed was nothing new to Kandan. In the eight villages around, whatever theft happened, Kandan and his friends would be arrested as suspects. As there was an ongoing friction between the police and the people of Perumanallur, they always found the least pretext to arrest one of them.

'What is this, Mr. Nagamalai? You seem to be simply drawing

Aagol | 115

lines in the register.'

Through the pillars of the façade of the police station, Usilampatti Deputy Magistrate Venkatesan moved as slowly as a temple car with his huge belly teetering in front of him. Nagamalai stood up and saluted him.

'Sit down! Is it black coffee? Order one for me too.'

Nagamalai asked Constable Mariappan to fetch black coffee.

'What are the Perumanallur folks telling?'

'Don't even ask me, sir. It is very difficult to make them understand.'

'It's ok if they don't understand Nagamalai. It would be tough only if they comprehend.'

'The village elders have gone to Madurai to give a petition to the collector. What will he do? Just embrace them and their petition huh?'

'Why should we be frustrated? If they don't agree, we have orders from the collector to arrest the whole village.'

'I am wondering, what is the government going to do with their fingerprints? Will they cook sweet *Pongal* with it? Where did this rule come from? Did it suddenly jump from the skies?'

'Nagamalai, this fingerprint law did not appear in the past few days. In 1860, in the northern part of India, a band of thieves were involved in minting forged coins. To curtail them, the Criminal Tribes Act was formed. In 1871 it was enforced. There are 31 Sections in it. Whichever community or caste involves themselves in theft or murder should be reported to the governor-general's advisory committee. Before that, the local government has to declare that the community or caste is a criminal tribe in the government gazette. If the governor-general approves of it then they would be categorised so.

'That caste crowd will be gathered at a particular place and monitored. Before that, the local government must create a scope or avenue for their livelihood. Only after that should the declaration be made. The declared caste people must all register their names with us. Otherwise, it would be a crime.'

One wonders if the black coffee came just when he finished or if he stopped right there on sighting it.

'Isn't it good news that if they register then they will be given food? It seems like a good law, magistrate. Why are these folks so uncooperative?'

'Nagamalai, there is an issue though. In 1911 they amended the law and changed many of the things that I have shared so far. Now, they have given the powers to the local government and the Zilla collector himself can identify a tribe or caste and declare them as a Criminal tribe. They don't have to get the approval of the governor-general. Additionally, the declared caste need not be provided with livelihood alternatives or any such sham. We just need to register their name, body identification, address, and ten fingerprints. They need to follow this till their death. They need to sleep in the government-assigned place, say the panchayat office verandah, or any other commonplace from 11 at night to 3 in the morning every day. The village would ring a bell and everyone has to get into their common bed. It is called the 'bell bed'. We hear this sound from the neighbouring village, right? That's what it is. You should tie the bell for your village.'

'Why do we have two registers, A and B?'

Venkatesan collected both the registers and kept them on his lap. He was stroking them as if they were twin babies. Then he explained.

'10-1-A should register all people who are above sixteen years old in the village, all of them. 10-1-B should register the people whom the local government suspects as prospective criminals. This is a special register for that. They are called KD which stands for Known Dacoits.'

'Ok. Let us take this Kandan. If he registers in this, then can he not go visit his native town's temple, Nattamakulam Adisivan temple? Should he not go to the temple festival?'

'Why not? There is a Raadhaari Cheetu inner permit, which he has to apply for. Once he gets it, he can roam around freely. But he cannot stay outside his village for more than 15 days.'

'This seems to be a convenient law, magistrate.'

'These savages will not understand. The home ministry had passed an order two years ago, according to rule 1331—*piramalaikallars* of Madurai zilla to be a criminal tribe. They have also placed their fingerprints. The whole of Madurai became quiet immediately. Why are these Perumanallur thieves clamouring?'

'One should handle this smoothly like dipping jackfruit in honey. They would listen if told properly. But I don't understand as to why they have appointed you as a special magistrate?'

Kottavi entered the police station with a goat kid.

'Aiya, Kottavi!'

'What? Have you come to help wash Kandan's arse?'

'Our Buffalo Chaser Aanguthevan sent this goat kid. It was grazing in the sugarcane plantations of the Big House. Please check if this is the kid you are searching for.'

The constable inspected the kid. It had the javelin seal on its face. Constable Mariappan pointed the seal to Nagamalai's face.'

'What? Do you want me to kiss the goat?'

'No! Ins Aiya, the javelin seal….'

'Hmmm…I saw…'

After crossing the tamarind tree near the police station, Kottavi screamed out the last line of his message.

'Aangu asked you to release his brother Kandan.'

Nagamalai got enraged. He threw his black coffee glass at Kottavi. It splattered on the tamarind leaves.

'Is your Aangu some British lord? What's with these guys, Kottavi, and whatnot? If you ever step into the station, I shall chop your head off like a sacrificial lamb! I warn you.'

The choultry was convenient enough for Govardhan to read the books that he had brought along. He had to make some policy decisions on heavy weapons and so he was reading up the files and some books about that. The choultry stood testimony to the fact that Nisha Pilot was an excellent artist. She had used bricks and coal to draw on the long walls of the huge *kottaram* (a huge hall with a top roof where many people can sit and eat together) The scenes that she observed in Perumanallur were depicted on the walls.

Pramil would normally be loitering the streets. He had befriended Karuvayan and Kottavi. Karuvayan had the job of unloading goods and distributing them in the Nadar shop in Vandipettai, Usilampatti. Pramil used to accompany him. He wanted to see a stage play and he was requesting Karuvayan about that. Karuvayan explained that a few years back a great famine had hit them and so many actors and musicians had died of hunger; some had moved away to Burma, Ceylon, and Penang. He also said that they had to travel to Madurai to see a play. The only storyteller of the village was Virumayakkal who sold buttermilk. He insisted that listening to her story was as vivid as watching a play.

There was a cow shed in the corner of the choultry. To accommodate the visitors, they had moved the cows elsewhere. There was a neem tree near the shed. Nithilan spent his time under the tree. In all times—past or present—he seemed to have a neem tree. He was watching the web series that he had downloaded on his laptop. He would also listen to his favourite number, 'Golden Girl' quite often. He would think of Senga, often. He would laugh with her, walk with her, and hug her; he would check on the tracker by monitoring his watch.

The common problem for the four of them was the lack of proper toilet facilities. They had to walk nearly three miles into the forest from the choultry and they found it difficult. A small platform was raised for a toilet between the bathroom and *erikuzhi* (a compost pit behind the house where they throw ash, cow dung, and vegetable waste), but it could not be used as a toilet because there was no running water or sewage. They enquired about this to Chinna Poojari, but he said that they should talk to Cheeni Thevan of the Big House to sort it out. Nithilan stepped out to the Big House that day.

'The fourth house is the Big House,' said an elderly man who was working on the organic fertiliser. Nithilan did not understand, why it was called the Big House. It looked like the rest of the mud houses of the village. The verandah was bigger. There was a green wooden gate that was painted with a peacock. Chinna Mayan was swinging on the gate.

'Nethili uncle.'

He called out cheerfully. Nithilan did not expect Chinna Mayan there. He held Nithilan's hands tightly and took him in.

'Welcome, Aiya'.

Chinna Mayan's mother Dhanam, welcomed him warmly. People were not living with the cattle inside the house. Apparently, the cattle lived in the house and the people also stayed there. Goats, cows, hens, three sisters of Chinna Mayan, two paternal uncles, maternal uncle, aunts, and their kids—all of them lived under one roof. As it housed so many people and livestock, it was known as the Big House, was Nithilan's surmise.

'Listen, Pothum Ponnu, get some buttermilk for this Thambi.'

'Oh! Please don't bother. That's alright. I came to meet Cheeni Thevan Aiya.'

'He has gone to help out with a calf at the Karuppan Kadu.'

Nithilan scratched his beard and stood hesitantly.

'Hey Chinna Maya, take Thambi to Aiya.'

Chinna Mayan agreed, nodded his head and tied his dhoti up. But it slipped and fell. The women in the house burst out laughing. Pothum Ponnu rushed to his assistance and tied up the dhoti for him.

Karuppan Kadu was about half a kilometre away from the Big House.

As it was a forest land that had grown around the Karuppu temple, the villagers had written the forest lands in the name of Lord Karuppan.

'Nethili uncle, what is the name of your village?'

'Bharat.'

'Where is it?'

'It is 110 years away.'

He nodded his head as if he understood.

'Did you come by ship?'

'We came by train.'

'How will a train be?'

'It will be big and shiny.'

'Will they sell fries like murukku in it?'

'Not murukku, but plenty of other snacks.'

'Do they stage plays in your village?'

'Many…'

'What roles will they play?'

'All of them will play many roles. Ok, now you answer my questions.'

'What are you going to ask?'

'Why is she called Pothum Ponnu? Is she your elder sister?'

'Yes, my third sister.'

'Why do they call her that?'

'They were having daughters consecutively. My Aiya wanted

a son. When he got the third daughter, he named her "Pothum Ponnu", meaning no more daughters. Then I was born!'

Nithilan was astounded by the faith that the family had in that name. He realised that faith is what makes the world go around.

'What is your father doing with the calf, Maya?'

'Ask this question to Aiya.'

'Do you like cows?'

'Yes.'

'Good. Cows are like gods. We need to always pray to them. They are like our family gods!'

'When a famine came in the village, they killed the cow for food. My mother said.'

'The government must take care that famines don't affect the land.'

'Does your land not have a famine? Will everyone get jeerani, all the time?'

'Ours is a developed nation. It will be like a temple.'

'Developed nation means building temple, eh?'

'You won't understand all this. Your later generation will understand all of this.'

Chinna Mayan gaped. They crossed a haystack. Something plopped on Nithilan's head. Nithilan groped around and picked it up. It was a one-metre snake. It was dust-coloured. His hands started shaking. Chinna Mayan took the snake from him.

'This is *Olavu* snake (sand boa). It won't bite.'

He put it across his neck.

When they entered the Karuppan Kadu, Cheeni Thevan, who was far away among the thick shrubs, signalled to Chinna Mayan, asking him not to approach.

A calf that had lost its mother, the orphaned calf needed milk and the mother's affection. So Cheeni Thevan was trying to pair it with another mother cow. It wasn't an easy task. The other mother must agree and the calf must cooperate.

He tied the calf to a tamarind tree and took the mother cow inside the forest. He inserted his hand into its anus and recreated the pain of delivery. When his hand reached the womb sharply the mother cow screamed as if it was in labour pains. At that moment he rushed and released the calf from the tamarind tree.

He smeared the mother cow's blood onto the calf. He then left the calf next to the mother cow. When the mother sniffed the birth smell, it started licking the calf. The calf happily started drinking its milk.

'Is it the foreign thambi? Come along. What is the news?'

'Aiya, we want a separate toilet room in the choultry.'

'We had spoken to the municipal authorities, Thambi.'

'Nothing materialised.'

'There is already a platform.'

'But there is no water or drainage system....'

'We will switch on the motor. We will ask them to dig a *thuppankuzhi*' (a hole through which the sewage water from the house can drain).

'Thanks, Aiya.'

'Thambi, how is your work coming up?'

'It's all going fine.'

'Are you missing any box in the burial grounds?'

Nithilan was flabbergasted. Which box? What is he saying?

'We have kept it at the panchayat office. Check it.'

Cheeni Thevan left accompanied by Chinna Mayan. Nithilan rushed to the panchayat office headlong. The box was in the middle of stacked paddy sacks. Nithilan covered his face with both hands and let out a huge sigh of relief. It was one of the boxes that Pramil had brought along. Pramil had not made any fuss over it and had not informed anyone that it was missing. Must be that innocuous a box! Yet, he carried it along and stepped out of the office. He went directly to the Usilampatti burial grounds. Mandayan was drinking his gruel outside his hut.

Everything was as it should be! He could see no visible damage done. Nothing was dug out. Ignoring the secrets buried underground, the skies were filled with carefree birds flying around.

World over, experts had been deputed in the various intellectual centres to combat the Jelly attack. Indian Institute of Technology, the Asian Technology Association, Anna University, and other huge technological organisations had all joined hands in creating 'counter Jelly' groups and strived to find a solution. A rumour was also floating that in China, they had already written a counter program to neutralise the Jelly.

A team was constituted under Mohan Janarthanan's lead in Sirrius. He was operating in a defence mode in the 'network negative' ecosystem to defend against Jelly. The Internet security team trained by Nithilan was writing many counter-effective programs.

After returning home Mohan wore the Meeta contraption on his head as usual. It was reassuring that the Meetaverse had not been corrupted by Jelly yet. He was building a general hospital in his imaginary city. He was creating mirrors of top medical experts, their traits, skills, and competencies. Patients in any corner of the world, with any kind of ailment, could get treatment there; with real-time knowledge and experience, he was creating the virtual hospital and was enhancing its path. Just like all the other people in his world, the doctors were also wearing dark glasses.

Machiavelli was sleeping. He was wearing the white clothes of a medico. He had a toy strung around his neck like that of a snake with a raised hood. Mohan was concerned that it might constrict his neck, and so he tried to remove it from his neck, but Machiavelli woke up then. He slapped Mohan's hands off his neck.

'It's a stethoscope. Don't touch it,' he instructed and rolled over.

'Drink your milk and sleep, Maci.'

He shut his eyes tight and screwed them up and posed as if he had already gone to sleep.

30

The identity of the girl who had fainted amidst the cacti was unknown. She resembled a white woman and they carried her to the choultry. Nithilan was acutely shocked. It was Senganthal. Before he could figure out how she appeared there, she regained her consciousness. Nisha Pilot gave her some water to drink.

Nithilan was getting ready to meet Cheeni Thevan to talk about the toilet facilities.

'I will also come with you.'

Senga held onto Nithilan's hands.

'You take rest. I shall finish the visit.'

She was not willing to listen to him.

Cheeni Thevan was not in the Big House. His wife Dhanam informed him that he was in Karuppan Kadu.

'Hey Chinna Maya, take Thambi to Aiya.'

Chinna Mayan agreed, nodded his head and tied his dhoti up. But it slipped and fell. The women in the house burst out laughing. Pothum Ponnu rushed to his assistance and tied up the dhoti for him. But she tripped and fell. Senganthal rushed to Pothum Ponnu's help and she also tied Chinna Mayan's dhoti.

Karuppan Kadu was about half a kilometre away from the Big House.

'Nethili uncle, what is the name of your village?'

'Bharat.'

'Did you come by ship?'

'We came by train.'

'How will a train be?'

'It will be big and shiny.'

'Will they sell fries like murukku in it?'

Nithilan smiled silently.

'They will sell their nations too, in their trains, Thambi!' interrupted Senga.

'Do they stage plays in your village?'

'Many...'

'What roles will they play?'

'Role of God! That is the trend across pan India.'

'What?'

'Senga, he is a small boy. Won't you speak something relatable to his times and age? Why are you dumping your social reform sewer on him? Chinna Maya, now you answer my questions.'

'What are you going to ask?'

'Why is she called Pothum Ponnu? Isn't she your elder sister?'

'Yes, my third sister.'

'Why do they call her that?'

'They were having daughters consecutively. My Aiya wanted a son. When he got the third daughter, he named her 'Pothum Ponnu,' meaning no more daughters. Then I was born!'

'Then they should have prayed for Venum Paiyan. (need a son) Why are they naming her Pothum Ponnu and torturing her?

Senga screwed Chinna Mayan's topknot.

'What is your father doing with the calf, Maya?'

'Ask this question to Aiya.'

'Do you like cows?'

'Yes.'

'Good. Cows are like gods. We need to always pray to them. They are like our family gods!'

'When a famine came in the village, they killed the cow for food. My mother said.'

Senga looked at Nithilan piteously.

'The government must take care that famines don't affect the land.'

'Does your land not have a famine? Will everyone get jeerani, all the time?'

Senga embraced Chinna Mayan and said, 'In our place, not everyone will get jeerani all the time. But the crores of people will get *halwa* quite often.'

They crossed a haystack. Something plopped on Senga's head. Senga groped around and picked it up. It was a one-metre snake.

'OMG! A cobra!'

Chinna Mayan ran away.

The snake stung on Senga's head. She was stunned and fell unconscious on the cacti plants nearby. A cigarette smell emanated from the bushes…

'Senga…. Senga….'

Nithilan woke up from his nightmare in great panic. Nisha Pilot rushed next to him and shook his shoulders to wake him up. Govardhan was standing right behind her with a lighted cigarette held in his fingers. Nithilan was slightly confused as to whether it was Pramil or Govardhan. Govardhan was wearing Pramil's shirt.

'Is Senga your friend? We could have brought her along with us. Now you relax.'

Govardhan reassured Nithilan calmly.

He had an itching sensation in the place where the snake had fallen on his head. He was worried if it was a sand boa or a cobra. When he enquired about it with Chinna Poojari, he recommended that he consult a physician. Karuvayan informed him that, *Silambu* (a traditional martial art played with bamboo staff) teacher, Vitti Vellaiya Thevar had an antidote for poison.

Kandan, who had been released from Sindhupatti prison had come to meet his elder brother Aanguthevan. They both had created a fire on the ridge and fried *kelathi* fish and discussed the happenings of the village over a meal.

'Why is Insu Nagamalai so irritated with us, Kanda? Did he say anything?'

'Our Nallur men have not registered their fingerprints yet. Madurai collector had insisted that we should register our fingerprints and had been pretty strict about it. Nagamalai was discussing this with yet another person. Just as Chinna Poojari parted his hair, they were drawing long lines in a notebook that the Ins had. It is still empty but for the lines was the sarcastic comment made by the man with a black gown.'

'They are called Magistrates. His name is Venkatesan.'

'I don't know what goat shit it is. Why should we register our fingerprint, Aangu? Are we stealing all day long?'

'You see, Kanda. The white policemen are unhappy with our watchmen's jobs. They said that it was wrong and we shouldn't take up these jobs. But we paid them no heed. If we are paid wages for watching over fields, they have declared that it is a crime. Still, none paid any heed. Now they are planning to register our fingerprints and keep us caged in the night.'

'Even if we were mere *vippu vavvals* (bats that are timid and completely harmless) the police would fear our existence and wet their dhotis! But if the police brand us as a criminal tribe, then none would fear us, Aangu.'

'What have you understood? They are serving the army men with plenty of eggs. The ones who were frail like eggshells are now strutting around like sturdy camels! They are lifting weights and developing rippling muscles. Our people who were grazing donkeys are now practising horse riding. They are given shooting practice by placing black cutouts of men. They are using our own hands to poke our eyes. This "divide and rule" has become their habit. The Sarkar (government) is working on crippling people like you and me. This is no joke, Kanda.'

'Whatever you say, Aangu, let us not agree to ever register our fingerprints. We have not committed any crime. If we bend our heads to them, that's probably the biggest crime that we would ever commit. We should never do that.'

Buffalo Chaser Aanguthevan patted Kandan's shoulders.

'You go see Vitti Vellaiya Thevar. He is very fond of you. Stay with him and make your living.'

Both rose and walked away from the ridge, went across the sugarcane plantation, crossed over to the south, and walked into Kodangi Street where their house was. Their mother Ponnamma was bedridden.

'*Aatha* (term for mother), Kandan has come. Police let him free because he has not done any crime.'

When the old lady heard Aangu's reassuring words, she shed tears.

The brothers' duo, prayed to their father Aanachathan's wooden staff, used for guarding fields, to get his blessings. Aangu lit a lamp next to it. He took a pinch of the sacred ash kept in a small pot and smeared it on Kandan's forehead. He spread some over his head.

31

The practice grounds of Vitti Vellaiya Thevar had a huge open space and a smattering of huts around. He was showing around his practice grounds to Nithilan and Pramil. Nithilan had come for treatment for the snake bite. 'You are the only person who has come for a treatment for a non-poisonous snake bite. It has just greeted you and gone,' commenting thus he spread some turmeric on his hand.

'This is the kids' hut.'

Village kids in the age group of eight, ten, and twelve were playing in the hut. Plenty of toys and playthings were piled in the hut. There were a whole lot of tops which were in a heap like guavas. Pramil picked a top.

'You are giving them training in traditional games like tops and *Pallankuzhi* (a traditional two-player board game) mancala. Why?'

'Why do you ask this, foreign Thambi? Do you think that they are just games? Playing with tops would teach them how to aim. It would calm the mind that is stormy like a cyclone. Snakes and ladders (*paramapadham*) would teach them that life is filled with ups and downs. Pallankuzhi will teach them to give wealth from where it is available to the ones who don't have it and will also teach them the concept of distribution of wealth. The throwing-stones-game will teach them alertness and strengthen their shoulder muscles. It would tone their arms for hard labour and farming. In my practice of skills, this is the mother of all other huts where skill sets are trained.'

There were plenty of huts where body-building exercises were taught and practised. There were buttermilk doling huts. In a big hall in the centre, mud was heaped up in the shape of a mattress.

On this mud mound, *sailathu* competitions were going on.

'What is it Aiya? They are practising without the *silambam* (stick), by just moving their arms.'

'That is sailathu, Thambi. It is to increase the speed in the movement of hands and legs, without the silambam. Our Kandan is an exponent at it.'

Kandan was defeating every opponent in the competition. He was very competent at his craft. 'If one could imagine that the players were carrying a silambam in their hands then it was an exhilarating spectacle of speed, movement, and dexterity,' suggested Vellaiya Thevar. Nithilan immediately jumped onto that imagination. In that figment of imagination, Nithilan's nose was broken by Kandan's silambam. He was bleeding profusely.

Kandan had defeated all the locals and Vellaiya Thevar embraced him in pride and praise. Thevar gifted him a silver chain. In the centre was a circular locket, with a peacock etched onto it.

Vellaiya Thevar sat on the rope-cot and the students sat on the ground with folded legs. He taught them breath control. Very soon the practice grounds became active with song, dance, theatrics, and games and were action-packed. Kandan served *pathaneer* (sweet toddy) in a small pot to Nithilan and Pramil. They didn't know how to quaff it and spilled it on their shirts.

'Should we now have a practice hut for quaffing toddy?'

Vellaiya Thevar was stroking his white beard and asked this in amusement.

Kandan narrated the experience he had in the prison. Vellaiya Thevar enjoyed the frankness with which Kandan said that they should protest against the fingerprint law, which seemed to be intensifying as the days progressed.

'Is this a new enmity, Kanda? In the year 1755, an English general named Colonel Heron was planning to destroy Koilkudi, near Melur. Our people considered it as our fort! He massacred plenty of people from our Kallar community. He stole our clan deity and took it to Tirunelveli. When he was on his way back our people were hiding in the Natham Pass and pounced on him and his army like lightning, beheaded them all and brought back our clan deity. Soon after in 1764, the English levied tax on our Kallar lands. The skies are generous with rains, the fields are giving harvest, why should we pay tax? Our fathers were very strong in their stand. They killed about 5,000 of our people for that. Since then and until now, there has been some friction or the other with them, isn't it? Today he is asking for a fingerprint. Tomorrow he may ask for our pupils!'

Pramil and Nithilan looked at each other.

Nithilan pondered if he should ask that question or not for a while and then he decided to edit a few words and persist with it.

'Please do not mistake me, Aiya. When you need to show some collective solidarity, is it good to talk about the pride of one's caste and stay as smaller groups?'

Vellaiya Thevar laughed out loud.

'What a comment you have passed! The Chozhas divided communities as left hand, and right hand into ninety-eight divisions. The right ones were farming caste. The left were merchants. The ones who did not fit into the right or left were the Kallar community. We did not bow down to the Mughal or Vijayanagar invasions. We have been independently ruling eight lands for many years now, for many harvesting seasons— Vaalaandhur, Thidiyan, Puthur, Papapatti, Karumathur, Kokulam, Veppanoothu, and Thummakundu. I am not talking about casteism but nationalism. Whatever I referred to are our gods, houses, lands, villages, grandfathers, great grandfathers and their lands, strength, staff, courage, pride, and arrogance. What else? If it seems like a mere caste issue for you, then so be it.

We are eighteen castes living together in these lands. Thambi, we have never had an inter-caste feud until now. The caste identity is huge, Thambi. But it is by itself! It is the ruling power that creates an explosion or infuses poison into it.'

Nithilan and Pramil thanked Vellaiya Thevar, bid their farewells to him, shook hands with Kandan, and took leave. They followed the same narrow path that the *kokkari* (oxen with horns bent forward) took for ploughing the fields and the two of them weaved their way back to the choultry.

'The same words.'

Pramil was talking to himself.

'Which words?'

'Pounced like lightning!'

'Yes. So what?'

'The Braganza letter, 1665, carries notes about the seventeenth century:

"*They went out of their woods in small bands, dispersed in the country under disguise, and were always ready to reunite at the first signal. The Kallans require only an instant to run like lightning....*

They went out of their woods in small bands, dispersed in the country under disguise, and were always ready to reunite at the first signal. The Kallans require only an instant to run like lightning...."'

'Oh....'

'Joseph Vieira, in his Madurai mission letter, had mentioned about fifty Kallars fighting against an army of 10,000 Mughals. There is a note about this event. They are not trumpeting their caste pride. Theirs is an ancestral pride. It's an absolute truth. A caste does not have separate pride, Nithilan. It is like a parasite that piggy rides on other's pride and heritage.'

'I feel that if we stay with them for some more time then we might become caste fanatics as Kallan, Maravan, Pallan, Paraiyar, Nadar, Vanniyan, the various castes, and more!'

'Why are you harping upon castes so much? As if Vellaiya Thevar is guilty of creating castes!'

'Ok! Then who invented castes?'

'The old man mentioned Koilkudi, right? That is the oldest community. Before the Aryans entered this land, the Tamil community lived as various tribes. Depending on the *thinai* (kinds of soil/geographical divisions) that they lived in, the Tamils were commonly identified as *kudi* (tribes), Eyinar, Kunra Kuravar, Kollai Kovalar, Andar, Ayar, Umanar, Pathavar, Uzhavar—were all Kudis. Amkudi, Mudhukudi, Kurambai kudi, Vettakudi, Neelkudi, Vizhukudi, Veezhkudi, Sezhungudi, Palkudi….the list goes on. The colonisation of India started with the coming of Aryans. Ever since they came, the kudi society became a hierarchical society. The thought that "People are high or low because of their birth"—this concept came into being. Portuguese gave our society, the name "casta". Then the British referred to caste, scheduled caste, criminal tribe, and so on. Now answer me, who invented caste?'

Nithilan pinched himself. This wasn't a dream. The person accompanying him on the walk was not Senganthal. Pramil was speaking as if he was Senga's partner.

When both of them crossed the Big House, they noticed Chinna Mayan's elder sister Pothum Ponnu sitting on the verandah and playing Pallankuzhi. If someone was worthy of being titled Miss Perumanallur it had to be Pothum Ponnu. The mole on the swell of her right cheek, her shell-like eyes which always looked as if they were yearning for something qualified for the title. Pramil was fond of her and Nithilan was aware of it.

'Pramil sir, are you not playing Pallankuzhi?'

'You see Nithilan, whatever you may say, in our timeline, she is my grandma. So, I don't want to play.'

'Shall we chase a crow and use 'Atharvana' to speak to Karthika, ma'am?'

'Ah! Nithi! Please keep quiet.'

Nithilan was singing Sanskrit carnatic songs. The kids who crossed them commented that they were some Vedic people.

'Sir, whom are they commenting about?'

'What?'

'Vedic people?'

'Ah, that one! We get food supplied from society, that Christian society. They are referring to them, not us. You continue singing.'

When they neared the choultry they found Nisha Pilot running towards them in her short skirt.

'Hey people, it is some good news. They have found a "kill code" for the Jelly. Your Sirrius team has cracked it. Ukraine engineers have assisted them. Linga asked me to convey that your "Nithilan Normal procedure" was extensively useful to them. Congrats!'

Pramil hugged Nithilan in joy.

'Everything is gradually returning to normalcy. Everybody is in data recovery mode. They asked us to be ready. Tomorrow we may get our network restored for our laptops. Linga is working on it. We may have to leave in four days.'

'Great! Where is Govardhan, sir?'

'The call went on for a long time. He had his dinner and retired.'

'We need to celebrate this great news with Chinna Mayan as the chief guest, and we should ask him to cut jeerani!'

The village became quiet by six in the evening. In many houses, they lit the hurricane lamps. When they opened the midriff of the lamps and poured kerosene, the glow became a beautiful gold colour. To take away the sharpness of the light they had placed a palm leaf on its wiring. The long shadows that were cast on the streets and the walls were used to scare the children to finish their meal. Some kids were playing out in the mud singing the folk song *Thirithiri Bommakka*. Kottavi was walking around with a shepherd's crook. Right in front of him and behind him, his flock of woolly sheep were following like the vestiges of the evening light.

The Karuppan Kattu owl seemed to be playing a game of Kabaddi with its eyes!

Someone had lit some camphor in the Kaliyamman ridge, and it was burning bright listening to the vibrant story that Virumayakkal was telling the kids.

The village was fast asleep.

The sound of the cows and bulls lapping water from the *kuzhithazhi* (mud tubs used for giving water to the cattle) also became quiet.

Other than the howling of the foxes, the air was still.

Other than the sheer darkness spread by the night, the streets were colourless.

In the river banks of Pannaipatti, a lone banyan tree was red. Someone lay on his tummy with his neck slit. His face was not visible in the dark. The fading moon ray, way past midnight, identified the man to be Kandan.

32

In the hall in front of the mortuary were present the Sindhupatti Inspector Nagamalai, Thirumangalam Sub-inspector Raja Desingu, Usilampatti division Collector Veerasamy and Usilampatti Sub-registrar Venkatesan. Madurai Collector Reilley had ordered that they had to enforce the fingerprinting law in Perumanallur. The power vultures had been frustrated with helplessness and they now found a reason—Kandan's corpse.

'Nagamalai, what sort of a person is Kandan?' enquired Veerasamy.

'They said he is a competent fighter. He was clinging on to the dhoti of that Vitti teacher and making his living. He has an elder brother, Aanguthevan. He is called the Buffalo Chaser by the villagers. Their father died in Penang. Their mother is bedridden.'

'He has been slit at his throat. Who would be his enemy in the village?' asked Venkatesan curiously.

'We are not sure. If you give us some time, we shall investigate.'

'Are you aware that the fingerprint collection agent would go into the village and gather all their fingerprints on the third of April?' asked Veerasamy.

'Aiya, we will get that job done, for sure.'

'As if you would, huh? If you give them a mere instruction to register fingerprints, they protest vociferously. I feel if you use Kandan's corpse as bait, then they may concede,' suggested Venkatesan.

'You are asking me to use the corpse? I don't understand.'

'First, instruct everyone that none should step out of the village for the next ten days. I will create a notice and place my seal of authority. Announce it as an order. Then ask the village drummers to follow it up with the announcement of registering the fingerprints. Ask them to inform with great emphasis that the ones who fail to register will be imprisoned.'

'We will execute all of that sir. But where does Kandan feature in all of this?'

'Warn them strictly that if they fail to cooperate, every villager, man or woman, would be brought to the police station for the inquiry of Kandan's murder. They would be stripped naked and hot iron rods would be inserted into their ass and the torture would go on!'

'This is good advice, Aiya.'

'Veerasamy Aiya, we can see it from another angle also. I heard that they are going to recruit people from the village for the position of CID. Kandan was in prison and then went into the village after he was released. If we can register him as a CID agent in the public register, then we can file the chargesheet as the murder of a government official. The crime would become larger. We need to dig a larger hole to make the people of Perumanallur concede,' commented Venkatesan.

'Well, well! If we do this the high command would also get suitably angry with the villagers. The deadline on third of April will be for additional people who are armed. We will get an additional resource of people and weapons too! We can kill our way through,' said Veerasamy confidently.

'Shooting them won't work, Aiya! Even if the local Sarkar keeps quiet the British man would question us,' chimed in Sub-inspector Raja Desingu.

'I was just thinking it through, Raja. If they do register the fingerprint, we are going to fraternise with them by partaking in the gruel with them. All this bravado is only until then,' Veerasamy pacified.

Aanguthevan was waiting outside to collect Kandan's body. His eyes had reddened with constant crying. He was seated in the verandah. He stuffed his dhoti into his mouth and sobbed inconsolably. He was trying to choke on his grief. He was nostalgic about his youthful days when he and Kandan led a carefree life, going on bat hunts. He heard it as an oracle from the sky, all over again, when his father Aanachathan had told him, 'Take care of your younger brother well.'

The elders and young ones of the village had gathered there. When Chinna Mayan found Aangu crying his heart out, he could not stop crying himself. His sister Pothum Ponnu hugged him to her chest. Her face and eyes were streaked with tears. Virumayakkal was beating her chest, slapping her head and wailing.

Karuvayan was holding on to Virumayakkal. Kandan's maternal uncle Mayandi Thevar was shouting, 'Come out, you police fellows!' Chinna Mayan's father Cheeni Thevan was pacifying him and asking him to keep quiet.

Nithilan was sitting with his laptop under the neem tree which was a few metres away from the mortuary. His connectivity to his current time was slowly getting restored. Although he was observing the activities around him, he could not relate to the rampant emotion of the village.

Inspector Nagamalai fixed his cap and stepped out.

'Collect the body in ten minutes. Who has come? Where are the relatives?'

Chinna Mayan pointed out Aanguthevan, who greeted Nagamalai.

'I want to announce to the village. For the next ten days, none should step out of this place. This is the magistrate's order. Your panchayat will get a notice from the collector tomorrow. In case anybody breaks the rule and steps out, I warn you, the punishment would be severe.'

Nagamalai got into the motor car and sped away.

None of the villagers were shocked by this declaration. Only Nithilan was astounded. It was 31 March. They need to travel to the future in barely four days. How could they stay here for the next ten days? Is the rule applicable only to the locals or to strangers too? When Chinna Mayan came rushing and tumbled on his lap, Nithilan forgot all the questions racing in his mind. He identified himself as a local. His laptop flashed an e-placard, 'Welcome to Sirrius stock,' just at that moment to negate this spot of happiness.

Kandan's relatives threw a handful of mud on his body and moved away, wiping their tears. To protect the corpse from being dug out and mauled by dogs or foxes, Aanguthevan placed the thorny branches of the jujube tree over the body and then filled it with mud. Mandaiyan slapped the mud around and evened the mound. That very night Aanguthevan tied his dhoti up and went about with his job of staying guard at the sugarcane plantation.

Nithilan, who returned to the choultry, conveyed Nagamalai's announcement to everyone. No one seemed unduly worried about it. Pramil had some indigestion because of the rice and meatballs that he ate and so he wanted to wash it down with buttermilk. They both enquired the way to Virumayakkal's house. She was lying on the raised platform of her front verandah.

'Sister!'

She rose immediately.

'Buttermilk?'

'Foreign Thambis? Had you asked for it I would have fetched it for you myself. Please come in.'

She rushed inside the house and lit a lamp. Nithilan and Pramil sat on the wooden cot which was resting on the wall. It seemed too fragile to hold their combined weight and so they did not want to risk it and sat down. Virumayakkal brought some buttermilk laced with chopped onions in small pots.

'Sister, is Kandan related to you?'

Nithilan could still hear Virumayakkal's loud sobs.

'Yes. He is my younger paternal uncle's son. I have hand-raised him by laying him on my lap, showing him the rattle and playing with him and narrating the story of Gadodgajan from the Puranas. He was a strapping young man. Someone jinxed him and he got his throat slit. Even though he is dead and buried, he still lives in my eyes.'

She started crying again. Pramil glared at Nithilan.

'Amma, please forgive us. We shouldn't have troubled you at this time of your mourning. We are grateful for the buttermilk you served. How much should we pay....?'

'There is no price for the buttermilk that you drink for your thirst, Thambi.'

Nithilan and Pramil were in an uncomfortable silence for a few seconds, not knowing what to say. Then they bid their farewell. Nithilan was keen on knowing the Gadodgajan story from Virumayakkal.

It had been a long time since Machiavelli had a cocaine lollipop. He had a toothache and so the dentist had advised him to go slow on sweets. He didn't go to school either. He was tested and it was diagnosed that he had spider fever. Mohan also took off from his work. Mohan felt that they seemed to have become lonelier in their isolation.

In those twelve off days, he created a modern police station in Meetaverse City. Just as there was a high beam of light on the top of the lighthouse, the modern police station had a monstrous eye of light that kept swivelling. It contained every book of every individual in the city. A book meant that ever since a person was born, until the person's current age whatever activities had happened would be registered and it would be an e-encyclopedia. The eye shed light across the city in such a way that it protected its citizens dearly. Machiavelli behaved as if he didn't like this form of the city; he was lying on his peacock mattress, pulling a sheet up to his nose. He had traces of trance in his eyes, not sleep though.

'Do we need this when there is so much grief and death in the village?'

There was a girl-seeing ceremony arranged, from Veerana Thevar's family, for Pothum Ponnu. The groom Nalluthevan was an army man. They had already had talks about it around January. No one expected this disaster and death to happen in the village. Cheeni Thevan was unwilling to push away the auspicious event of his house.

'It's all right, Dhanam. Let them come and see the girl. It is not as if we are going to cut the goat and cook a feast and put up the *panthal* (a temporary shed for conducting marriage or other events). Pothum Ponnu is like a young palm tree. We can't push her wedding for too long.'

'There are two elder sisters who are not living with their husbands. What is the rush to get the youngest married?'

'I am hoping that at least this arrangement will be perfect and work in our favour. We will pray to Nattamakulam Adhishivan. We will pray that we will tie sugar cane for the temple festival. Let things happen as they are destined, my dear.'

The Big House was seeing a lot of activities and a feast was getting ready: vegetable gravies, dried vegetables, pappad, pickles, marinated fries, vadas, fruits, and dosas; there were more than eighteen items in the feast. The stoves and urns were wafting with the aroma of great food cooking.

Koni, the cow, was constantly mooing. No one had time to take care of her. Chinna Mayan rushed with Nithilan. Nisha Pilot joined them.

'The cow has a poisonous tooth. It is a long one behind the molars. The tooth needs to be razed down in its length. Or it should be made to bite an iron rod and that tooth will break and crush to pieces. Instead, if someone keeps shoving hay in its mouth, what will it do?'

Virumayakkal gave these details to Chinna Mayan.

Chinna Mayan held Koni's jaw, opened it and inspected it. Just as Mayakka had predicted, it was the case of a poisonous tooth. He searched for an iron rod. As the house was buzzing with the auspicious event, he couldn't find one in the house; things had been moved around. Chinna Mayan scratched his head and wondered.

'What do you want, Mayan?' asked Nithilan.

'Iron rod. If I give it to the cow to bite, the tooth will crack and explode.'

He ran around searching for one.

'You need iron. It could be anything, right?'

'Yes, but it has to be in the size and shape where the cow can bite.'

'Nisha, can you give me your pistol?'

Nisha smiled, checked if the gun was locked and handed it over to Nithilan.

'This is also iron.'

Chinna Mayan took the pistol and shoved it into the mouth of the cow. She tried to bite it hard and spit it. The poisoned tooth cracked and crumbled in that one bite!

Though the arrangements for the 'girl-seeing' ceremony were going well, Kandan's death was haunting like a layer of *puttama* (talcum powder) on everyone's face. Nithilan wanted to wipe it clean. He played his favourite song, 'Golden Girl' on his laptop and amplified it on his bebop speakers. The young girls who were assisting in the makeup of Pothum Ponnu, lining her eyes with kajal were teasing her saying, 'The song is played keeping you in mind!' Virumayakkal chased them away and accused them of being jealous girls.

'Why are you crying, dear?'

Pothum Ponnu looked wan and listless. Her kajal was melting down as black streaks of tears. Virumayakkal was the only one who observed Pothum Ponnu's sadness.

'I don't want this marriage, Mayakka.'

'What are you saying dear?'

The conversation that ensued, went on for some time, and at the end, Virumayakkal stepped out bearing the shock of the news. Pothum Ponnu stood there without even wiping her tears.

Veerana Thevar's family arrived in fancy bullock carts. Everyone would be served vegetarian food, considering the auspicious nature of the event. But the groom Nalluthevan will be served meat and rice. They would serve a heavy meal and

Aagol | 147

Cheeni Thevan and his family would check if he was up to it, to gorge on a heavy feast, as this was an important qualification to turn into a groom. They were determined to check that out.

'Whatever you may say, none can eat like Gadodgajan, right?'

Having uttered this comment, Chinna Mayan twirled his non-existent moustache.

'The groom hasn't set his eyes on the bride yet. When will that happen?'

Nisha Pilot boxed Chinna Mayan's ears and asked him.

'As if she is some pretty thing, and someone must see her, eh?'

'Hey! You don't know how many fans are there in this village for your sister. The fan club leader is staying with us in the choultry.'

Nithilan defended Pothum Ponnu. Before he completed his statement, Pothum Ponnu arrived with a tray of glasses of milk. Veerana Thevan's relatives welcomed her warmly and then inspected every inch of her keenly. She ran inside the house with her head bent. Chinna Mayan brought the two glasses of milk left on the tray that she had brought and served to Nithilan and Nisha. The elders moved on with discussions about the next move and the talk also touched upon the topic of fingerprint registration law.

'We met the collector and gave him a petition. If there are thieves, keep us informed and we will find them for you, but we can't register our fingerprints, is what we have informed categorically. We are hoping that the collector will give us the good news. We have prayed to Karuppan. Let us wait and watch.'

Veerana Thevar sounded confident. Cheeni Thevan held his hands. Nalluthevan was trying to catch a glimpse of Pothum Ponnu once more, but he did not succeed amidst the crowd around him. The girl's family was enjoying this failed attempt.

The elders kept chatting for a long time and so Chinna

Mayan fell asleep on Nithilan's shoulders. As usual, his dhoti came off. Nisha was trying to tie it for him. Nithilan stopped her as he observed something around his waist. A silver chain was tied around his waist. A circular locket, with the etching of a peacock, was visible. Vitti Vellaiya Thevar had gifted it to Kandan.

00000000034

Many long years ago, Eriveerampatti was ruled majestically by Peyandi Raja, who was armed with a woolen blanket, a jug, a cane, wooden clogs, and a spittoon. In the Tamil month of *Aippasi* (mid-October to mid-November) there was torrential rain with a bleating noise in his guava orchards. After the rains, the orchards were filled with goats, sheep, and woolly sheep and their kids. They later realised that God had sent a goat in every raindrop. The king was elated. But the sheep and goats grazed and foraged every leaf, branch, and fruit. The orchards dried up. The next morning when Peyandi Raja woke up, he found that the goats and sheep had been killed and eaten by hyenas. Now the king had lost the sheep and goats and the orchards and was worried. He went to the mutt of Visaga Digambarar and asked him for advice. 'I have a watchman. His name is Beeman. He will come to your orchard and keep watch for you,' said Digambara Sami. Beeman, who was as tall as seven horses piled one on top of the other, came to keep watch. After that, the goat-sheep rain never happened in the orchards. The guavas grew round and ripe and the orchard was laden with fruits. The mystery befuddled the king. So, he sent the rabbit-eared fruit bat to spy over the orchard. The bat hid himself in the tree and scouted the territory. That *Aippasi* month it started raining again. A man who was as sturdy as the Muruga Mountain came into the forest. He was Beeman's son Gadodgajan. When it rained, bunches of goats and sheep fell. Gadodgajan opened his mouth wide and swallowed all of them and kept them in his stomach. He sold it to the king of the neighbouring land called Ettabommu and earned plenty of gold and precious gems. His dad Beeman was aware of it, but he did not reveal it to anyone. The rabbit-eared fruit bat shared this story with Peyandi Raja and whined and sniffled about the betrayal. The king again went to Visaga Digambara Sami and complained. Digambara Sami asked him just one question. After that, the king never said anything and kept quiet and let it be.'

'What was the question, Virumayakkal?'

'Gadodgajan, who swallowed the goats and sheep, is he a thief? Or, you who are greedy to have both the orchards and goats for yourself are a thief?'

Nithilan wondered if Peyandi Raja would have understood the import of the question. He also desired to know what explanation Virumayakkal would give the children if they raised the question. But he hadn't come for that.

Nithilan was shocked to see the silver dollar peacock chain around Chinna Mayan's waist.

Before he could question Chinna Mayan about it, Virumayakkal rushed and picked the boy up. Nithilan noticed a secret panic in her face. On the pretext of hearing the Gadodgajan tale, Nithilan came to Virumayakkal's house, but he wanted to enquire about the chain.

'Sister, I thought they would put Gadodgajan behind bars.'

'Ask what you came here for, Thambi.'

The flashback went thus: Virumayakkal was to have married Cheeni Thevan. They had even been engaged, but at the time of marriage, she had been affected by tuberculosis. Soon after Cheeni Thevan married Dhanam, her disease was cured. Her amicable relationship with Cheeni Thevan's family continued to date. Dhanam, who was Cheeni Thevan's wife, allowed this relationship to continue without any rancour and was quite affectionate herself. Chinna Mayan and Pothum Ponnu were virtually Virumayakkal's children.

'You wanted to enquire about my children, right?'

'The chain around Chinna Mayan's waist?'

'Pothum Ponnu gave it to him, Thambi.'

'What are you saying sister? It is Kandan's chain.'

'Yes, Thambi. Kandan was devoutly fond of Pothum Ponnu. She was also very fond of him. He gave her the chain just before his death.'

Were Pothum Ponnu and Kandan lovers? If one were to slit open Gadodgajan's stomach many goats and sheep will pop out, similarly the chain that Vitti Vellaiya Thevan gave seems to have many secret tales buried within. Nithilan was dazed.

'Is that why she was so sad? Then she may know who killed Kandan, right?'

'That foolish girl would not know all of that.'

Nithilan firmly believed that she would know. The silver chain had exchanged hands within a night. The murder had also happened the same night. Then the murderer's face is likely to be hidden in the chain. Nithilan believed it to be a sure possibility.

'Was there anyone else in this village who was interested in getting married to Pothum Ponnu?'

'The whole village had an eye on her. Karuvayan has evil eyes. He had an *avagachi* (unsatiable lust over the desired object like land, woman, or money) on her.'

Nithilan walked towards the Kaliyamman ridge and saw the light of a distant lantern. That was Chinna Mayan. He was carrying a tiffin box. Aanguthevan had returned to the village that night, after the police interrogation. In this context it may not be safe for Chinna Mayan to go into the sugar cane plantation all by himself is what Nithilan thought cautiously. He accompanied Chinna Mayan and collected the tiffin box from his hand.

Nithilan was singing songs to dispel the fear of darkness. Till then, Chinna Mayan, who was brave, found Nithilan's singing to be scary.

They reached the temporary shack of Aanguthevan. It was

midnight and steadily growing dark. Aangu had wrapped himself with his blanket and with his staff in hand, he was walking around. The smell of food from the tiffin box grabbed his attention and he turned around.

Aangu had downed fermented toddy which had a high level of intoxication. He had lit a small fire to cook meat and Chinna Mayan went inside the shack and sat next to the fire to warm himself up.

'My deep condolences on the death of your dear younger brother, Aangu.'

Nithilan did not know how else to start the conversation. Condolences to Aangu sounded like esoteric pompous words in a government document, empty and meaningless. He turned his face aside.

'I don't have anything to give you foreign lord. This tiffin box rice won't suit your palate. Shall I have it?'

He was famished. Toddy and rice went in and converted his grief into tears and sweat and he poured them out. He started sobbing. Nithilan was not acquainted well enough to console him. But Nithilan could not bear to be silent.

'I have heard that your brother was a gentleman. None believed that he would have an enemy. Do you believe that the police would have had a hand in this?'

Aanguthevan rose in a rush and went inside his shack. Nithilan followed him. Aangu used his staff to remove the towel covering his rope cot. There was a blood-stained dagger hidden underneath.

'This….?'

'Found it on the banks of the Pannapatti. This is Kandan's dagger. The murderer has used Kandan's dagger to finish him.'

'Why did you not inform the police?'

'Sami, Kandan thought that even if we were to lose our lives, we should not bend our will to register our fingerprints. The village is also firm on this opinion. If I gave this to the police, then in the name of finding the fingerprint embedded in this dagger they would insist on taking the fingerprints of everyone in the village. They will then follow this line of thought and bother us each day, asking about fingerprints. It would be like us feeding the perverted group.'

'Do you think that we can stop them from implementing the act, by just hiding the dagger?'

'I do not know about that. But if you make some effort, you can stop it.'

'Me?'

'You have come from abroad. You are wise enough to discriminate right from wrong. You can speak in the Sarkar language. If you choose to, you can eradicate this Act.'

Nithilan happened to remember Home Ministry's Secretary Linga's warning about not getting involved in anything that happened in the village.

'No.... Aangu...we can't intervene in that. If we do... we would be...'

'Tell me, Aiya.'

'You won't be able to understand. I don't understand myself.'

Nithilan stared keenly at the dagger. There was a shred of flesh attached to the tip of the dagger. He did not want to investigate the dagger any further.

He mentally made up not to involve himself with Kandan's murder. His inner mind said that it was not wise to get close to anyone in the village. His mind's lotus shut its petals and closed down.

Chinna Mayan handed over the lantern to Nithilan, held his hands tightly, and walked along. Nithilan could not extricate his hand from the childish pressure.

00000000035

Aanguthevan's people had stolen the catalium container boxes and stored them in the train that brought food grains from Burma to Madurai. They had covered the boxes with gunny sacks just as the food grains were covered. Kottavi and Karuvayan were guarding the boxes. Nithilan was waiting with Inspector Nagamalai in the Madurai railway station to catch them red-handed.

The first person to step out of the train was Senganthal.

'Back home at least, they sold Adayal data in WhatsApp for ₹500. But now, you have trivialised it to the range of selling ginger coffee on the train!'

Nithilan scratched his beard. Pothum Ponnu, Aanguthevan, Kottavi, and Karuvayan followed Senganthal—they all stepped out of the train.

'These people do not have the strength to steal as much as you have factored, Nithi. They are exhausted. They are naïve. The Britishers' law has tied their hands and is waiting to whip them, right at their doorsteps. These people are not even aware of where you have descended from, and can't figure out if you are a foreigner or an alien! If it is possible, do some good for these people.'

As soon as Senganthal finished talking, a cobra fell on her head. She went into the forest and fainted on a cacti patch. Finally, he realised that he was only dreaming; Nithilan woke up calmly.

His conscience pricked that he must meet Pothum Ponnu one last time. When he ran it by Pramil, he was angry and stopped him from doing so.

'Nithi, did we come here for this? Don't you have anything better to do? What do you think of yourself? Do you want to stay back in this village and become an acclaimed caste leader?'

Nisha Pilot patted Pramil's shoulder and tried to calm him down. The room was still and silent for some time. Nithilan knew that Pramil himself would break the silence.

'I want to see Karthika badly, Nithilan. I must adopt a baby as quickly as possible and please her. I am pissed off with any thought other than this.'

Tears welled up in his eyes.

'We shall go, sir. In a matter of two days, 'Veer Jadayu' would be here. We have taken special permission from the deputy collector to leave the village despite the ban imposed by the police. We shall leave.'

The drummer was making some announcements in the street.

'The announcement is for the residents of Perumanallur.

Coming third, in the presence of the police officials, people who are above the age of 16 must gather on the Nallur grounds and register their names, addresses, and ten fingerprints. From the fourth, every evening, they have to place their fingerprints in the panchayat and public office registers. They must sleep where the police officials order them to sleep in the night. Sarkar has brought this law for the security and protection of this village. The villagers are asked to cooperate. This is the collector's order.'

He banged on his drums and moved to Mel Street to make the announcement. Kottavi, who was sweeping the street, screamed, 'Go back home, you are a mere piece of white garlic!' and swept the street clean off the garbage and the drummer. The villagers complemented Kottavi as, '*Adichanda Bathar Vella*' (a comment of praise credited to Katta Bomman, who praised his warrior Vella Thevan) to mean that it was a smart observation. They applauded loudly and cheered for him. The drummer could not go to the other streets because of the crowd and so returned. The people who wanted to boycott the law did the preliminary boycott of chasing the announcer and the announcement.

36

Pothum Ponnu was sitting on the river bank. Chinna Mayan was keeping her company. He was living in his dream world where he was imagining being Peyandi King, having his royal staff, represented by a neem stick, looking up at the skies and awaiting the goats.

Nithilan had promised Chinna Mayan that he would show him cartoon films on his laptop. Nithilan had downloaded Kutti Raman's episodes and went in search of Chinna Mayan at his house and was informed that he was at the river bank. Nithilan arrived at the river bank and screened the cartoon to Chinna Mayan who was thrilled to see the animated pictures. He had not seen any pictures other than what his elder sister Pothum Ponnu drew. He was awed when he saw human figures walking and talking, flying monkeys, opening seas, magical forests—a whole world of fantasy. When Nithilan placed the laptop on Chinna Mayan's lap, he felt delighted that the gadget had finally lived up to its name.

'Pothum Ponnu?'

When Nithilan called out her name, she rose and hurried to hide behind the peepal (sacred fig) tree. She peeped out of it in a scared manner. Nithilan did not desire to investigate the murder by slowly collecting one clue after the other. He decided that it was an unnecessary chapter in his diary of this journey. But he yearned to know at least the name of the murderer before he left to his current times.

'Don't be scared. Consider me as your elder brother and please come out.'

Nithilan called out for the truth in her to come out!

She walked so quietly towards Nithilan that even her bangles did not clink. She stood next to him with her head bent. Nithilan used two fingers and delicately lifted her jaw and looked at her eyes, which were tearing up.

'They said that you were fond of Kandan.'

She unwound all the tears that she had bundled up so long. Nithilan folded his arms and waited for her to have a good cry. Each drop of tear seemed to carry the memory of Kandan and finally, when she wiped her eyes clean, she seemed to move on to the present day from the nostalgia of Kandan.

'I guess you know who killed Kandan.'

She nodded her head without any hesitation.

'Who?'

'Brother, what are you going to do about it, if you know the name, now? Can we bring Kandan back from the burial ground?'

He heard Pothum Ponnu talk for the first time. That one word 'brother' made him shed about a hundred and ten years and he was so moved emotionally that he could relate to her world.

'Pothum Ponnu, the man who committed a crime must be punished. Kandan was particular that we should not have the fingerprint registration law enforced. Now they are using his death to expedite that. We should not let that happen.'

'Brother! What are you saying?'

'Some random policeman has killed Kandan and is blaming one of the villagers; now they are using this as an excuse to summon everyone publicly and want to implement the fingerprint registration law. This is my surmise. The stubborn crowd that was resisting, is forced to concede because of a suspicious death. To tell the truth, I am suspicious of Inspector Nagamalai only. It's him, right? Tell me, it's him.'

'No, brother.'

'Is it Karuvayan? Be bold!'

'I don't need the courage to tell you. You probably may need the courage to hear it and process it.'

'What are you telling, my dear?'

'The person who murdered my Kandan is one among you, who stays in the choultry.'

Nithilan's head exploded as if a bomb had been dropped on the oleander flower. He staggered back and supported himself by leaning on the peepal tree. In Kutty Raman's story, baby Hanuman was carrying the Sanjeevi Mountain and flying. It seemed as if the mountain accidentally fell on Nithilan's head. He was completely stunned. Should he believe what she claimed or not? Is it something that did not happen or is it a truth that is better off, if unrevealed? Can a one-time-span kill another? It took Nithilan a few minutes to come out of his bewildering questions.

Nithilan pulled out his mobile and selected a groupie of his team. He enlarged Pramil's face and showed her.

'Was it him?'

She said that it was not him.

He pinched the photo back to its size. Pothum Ponnu looked at the groupie keenly and pointed her finger at Govardhan.

'What are you saying? Was it him?'

She said yes angrily. The midnight murder scene exploded into smithereens in her eyes.

Govardhan desired and lusted after Pothum Ponnu ever since he landed in Perumanallur. He wanted to enjoy every part of her to his heart's content and had been awaiting the opportunity with lascivious thoughts in his mind. He tried to accost her a few times. Knowing about Karuvayan's love for Pothum Ponnu, Govardhan would instruct him to describe her in minute detail, every time he came to the choultry, bearing food. Govardhan relished and revelled in the description. Govardhan was cautious that his team should not get wind of his desire and so stayed away from them and their activities. He used his army position as a cover for his isolation.

Pothum Ponnu was waiting secretly at the bank of the Pannapatti River for Kandan. Govardhan was smoking his cigarette in another corner of the bank. Just when he decided to advance on her, Kandan reached the place. Govardhan hid behind the bushes. Kandan spent a long time talking to her. He gifted the silver chain that he received from Vellaiya Thevar to her and tied it around her hand. He held her in a tight embrace and planted a kiss. When he attempted to overstep, she pushed him away. He came to his senses and took leave of her. The same night, on the same bank, Pothum Ponnu was sitting alone for the second time.

Govardhan came out of his hiding approached his dream girl and spewed cigarette words at her. He hugged her violently without her consent. He tried to undrape her sari and touch her skin. Pothum Ponnu struggled to escape his advances. With no choice left she screamed 'Karuppan!' for help. Kandan, who was walking in the distant fields, heard her shout for help. He rushed to her. He gave one sharp kick to Govardhan. He banged on the drumstick tree and crashed down. Kandan pulled out the dagger that he had tucked in his waist and tried to chop Govardhan's head. There was a long tussle between the two of them. Eventually, Govardhan used Kandan's dagger to slit his throat. Kandan fell and writhed in pain and died. Govardhan used the blood-stained dagger to twirl his moustache in victory and then threw the dagger away. Pothum Ponnu closed her mouth with her sari and sobbed inconsolably. Govardhan used wild animal energy to embrace her again. She held his shirt collar and shook him. He shrugged her hands off and kicked her stomach with his booted feet. She screamed in pain and fell and rolled up as a coil.

'If you report this to anyone, I warn you, your brother Chinna Mayan's head will not be there!'

Govardhan growled the threat under his moustache and returned to the choultry. Pothum Ponnu was in no position to seek help. She did not have the strength or the mind, to drag Kandan to the forest and bury him all by herself. She knelt next to his body, picked his right hand, and held it close to her chest. She stroked him affectionately and shut his eyes close. She left her love for him to guard his body and returned home.

What could one do with one's overwhelming emotions? One could allow it to ebb and flow and leave it to its course. One could restrain and bottle it and be plagued by it as a disease. Or one could objectively stand out and view one's emotions as a spectator.

Nithilan chose the third mode. But he was not blessed with the boon of being a mere spectator.

Karuvayan brought the chicken gravy vessel and kept it on the floor. Nisha Pilot poured it to other vessels.

'Hey Karuvaya! What are you people going to do on the third?'

Govardhan enquired while munching on the liver.

'What are you asking us to do, Aiya? We need to stand as *kiruthanukku maruthana* (be smarter than the smartest) and get our job done.'

'What do you lose by registering your fingerprints? Why don't you cooperate?'

'Aiya, it is not so simple! They are branding our whole community as thieves and asking us to register our fingerprints. That is wrong. Only if a person steals, he can be called a thief. How can he be a thief from his time in the womb? Just to enable the police sniffer dogs to catch us, can we earn our living right under their noses, to facilitate them? Is that why we have a government? A king enables food for hungry people. Is it the job of a king to be a mere monitor?'

Just as a full-bloomed flower's shadow falls on the river very gently, Karuvayan's indignant question found a shadow in Govardhan's times too and this realisation brought a smile to Govardhan's face.

'It's not just that, Aiya. We should sleep in the places that they assign during the night. Many villagers here go for night guard in the fields. Others work as daily wagers. Only if they work, can they make their living, and get food on their plate. If all the men are asked to report at the Panchayat and public offices who will do their jobs? If the government offers compensation as wages or food grains, then we can consider it, but they are declining to do so. This is *thalaperattu* (complete cheating), how can we accept this?'

Karuvayan did not stop there.

'Kandan died. They are now setting a narrative that he was a police spy and are provoking the high command to increase the number of armed people entering the village on the third. More pistols will be in the fray. Kottavi told me of this and this cannot be accepted.'

Nithilan entered the choultry when Karuvayan was finishing his last line. He sat right in front of Govardhan. He stared at him. Govardhan who was sitting with his legs crossed, uncrossed them and sat straight. He squirmed a little under the direct stare of Nithilan. Karuvayan's bullock cart left the choultry.

'Hey, Nithilan! What is it? Why are you staring at me?'

Govardhan could not handle the heat of the stare. Pramil was slurping on the chicken gravy and asked, 'What happened, Nithi?' Pramil's tone was laced with the spicy gravy.

'Govardhan sir, you should have killed Pothum Ponnu also, when you killed Kandan.'

'What rubbish are you blathering, Nithilan?'

'Even though she is alive, she is like the walking dead—a

zombie! I am not going to squeal about this to the villagers or the police. If I did, it would be a huge blemish and dishonour to our nation, sorry, our times! But my question is very simple. To compensate for the huge sin that you have committed, you must do some good to this community. You must! So, what will you do?'

'What's going on here, Nisha? What's wrong with him?'

Govardhan rolled his eyes and regained his old demeanour.

'I read about the Perumanallur riots. I read that nearly sixteen people were killed. They had even erected a pillar in memory of the dead. But the murder that you committed is going to change history. I heard what Karuvayan said. Additional guns, additional bullets, additional deaths! It could be anyone. It could be Chinna Mayan, Pothum Ponnu, Cheeni Thevan, Karuvayan, or anyone else. What you did is not just a murder, sir—but one that is going to cause a ripple effect and end up in a series of murders here. And because of the many who are going to die, we are going to lose them and their accomplishments in history.'

Nisha Pilot, who was frying chicken livers looked at Govardhan. He averted his eyes and was lighting a cigarette.

'We cannot change this law. But we can stop the riots. We must too! That would be the atonement we pay for your murder. We just have one more day left. Day after tomorrow, the officials would enter the village.'

'If you speak one more word, I shall kill you like how I stamped that fox to death in the forest!'

The heat of the words stuck Nithilan as if he was marked by a cigarette stub. He rose and pounced on Govardhan. In a split second, Nisha Pilot stopped frying chicken livers and punched Nithilan on his face and abdomen. He rose again and raised his hand; Nisha pulled him by his legs and banged him on the wall. Her boots were crushing his throat. Nithilan struggled to breathe. His eyes popped out. Pramil tried to stop Nisha and failed.

'Nisha!'

When Govardhan called she slowly removed her foot. Nithilan could not bear the stench of dominance from her footwear and so he coughed and choked. He slid down the wall and sat on the floor. His nose was bleeding and his face was sweating. He didn't feel like wiping both.

Just then 'Atharvana' called. Govardhan switched it on. Linga started talking.

'Linga from Bharat.'

'Tell us, Linga, Govardhan here.'

'Sir, tomorrow evening at exactly 7, 'Veer Jadayu' will land there. This time there is no scope for the time variable bug. In the under-universe track, it will come to and halt at the same place it dropped you earlier. Jaishankar's team will escort you. The PMO command is that you need to return tomorrow, positively, with the 2,000 boxes.'

'Command received, Linga. We shall come. How is the situation there?'

'All good, sir. The value, need and significance of the Adayal data is growing every millisecond.'

'We shall be back tomorrow, Linga!'

'Welcome back, sir!'

The call was disconnected and Nithilan was looking at them like a wounded animal. He was still.

Govardhan, Nisha, and Pramil started packing their things. Govardhan poured the chicken gravy into a small pot and started drinking straight. He bit into the chicken leg and relished it. Nisha Pilot served some liver on a plate to Nithilan. He didn't utter a word. Pramil placed his hand on Nithilan's shoulder. He did not respond. Everyone went about their chores busily and Nithilan just said:

'I am not coming!'

Aanguthevan and Nithilan had finished drinking the highly fermented toddy and were strolling on the Karattu Ridge. Nithilan did not feel like walking straight because he feared that his eyes would spill the truth. He desired to cross Perumanallur by train as effortlessly as he would go past the rains. Virumayakkal's tales, Vellaiya Thevar's narration of history, Aanguthevan's brotherly affection, Pothum Ponnu's unrequited love—all of these are meaningless in his life. This is what Nithilan needed to convince himself with and he threw stones aimlessly from the ridge. His thought process circled his apartment, the hungry kids, and that he must hurry back to cook food for them. He yearned for the moments when he would lose out on a conversation with Senganthal. Though he told his team 'I am not coming,' resolutely, in his mind, he was getting ready to go.

'Aiya, why are you so dull and listless?'

'What are your plans for the future, Aangu?'

'Plans are made by the government. Eating and guarding are our job.'

'What if this keeping-a-watch job is not there, tomorrow? Two days ago, the policemen entered the village and questioned the Nayakars why they were giving the job of watchmen to the Kallars. Kottavi gave me this information. If this goes on, what will you do?'

'We will engage ourselves in ploughing and sowing seeds, Aiya.'

'If the government orders you to go away from the fields, then what will you do?'

'My God Karuppan himself does not have the right to expel me from my fields, foreign Aiya! Where do the collector and the government have a place here?'

'Will you register your fingerprint, tomorrow?'

'The collector of Madurai feels that the village cannot be sent to prison and so he is turning the village itself into a prison. How will that work?'

'When you meet the officials tomorrow, what would be your standpoint? What will be your side of the story?'

'What standpoint are you referring to, Aiya? Would they even listen to us? We just received a tip, Aiya! The armed forces have arrived at Thirumangalam and shall move to Perumanallur and they are going to tie the villagers to a tree and forcibly register their fingerprints. The forces will walk down from Thirumangalam and stay overnight at Thummagundu and by dawn, they will surround Nallur. The deputy collector of Usilampatti and the magistrate are going to join the police forces via Kanniyampatti. Impotent folks!'

Pramil came and stood under the Karattu Ridge.

Nithilan took leave from Aanguthevan by embracing him.

Pramil informed that the peepal trees in the borders of the village were stained red with betel-leaves-juice-spit on them. He added that it was a warning to the officials that if the police entered forcibly, it would be a blood bath. On his way there, Pramil had also seen country bombs getting prepared. In case, the local villagers are unable to face the police force they would seek help from the neighbouring villages of Kalappanpatti, Kanniyampatti, and Murugampatti, and use the country bombs to protect themselves. Karuvayan had further informed them that at the Karuppu temple, many weapons like spears, short daggers, sickles, and stones to pelt had all been stashed secretly.

'Let all of it happen, Nithilan. Let the ones who die, die! I have read what you read too. It is the truth that sixteen of them died. It turned into a big news. It was debated in the parliament of London. It wasn't just that. The next year, in 1921, the British government's revenue department set up Kallar Reclamation Schools. These people came out of their violent ways. They were educated and their lives changed. In present-day India, in our society today, many of the Kallar community people hold high positions and command respect and esteem. This progress and growth were possible because sixteen people sacrificed their lives. Do not avert the sacrifice and stop the progress.'

Nithilan gave a fermented toddy grin to Pramil.

'Pramil sir, we have a future to console us about 110 years later. What consolation can we offer to people who are going to die here tomorrow?'

Nithilan held Pramil's gaze while they walked along. Pramil stared down at the red path while walking along.

They waited at the rock construction in the Usilampatti burial ground. The 2,000 boxes were dug up and stacked and were ready to be uploaded in 'Veer Jadayu'. As the boxes were buried for some time, they were covered with mud and spoke tales of mud. Nithilan was troubled because he would not be able to take a proper farewell from Chinna Mayan. When he researched on his laptop, he found Chinna Mayan's name also on the pillar erected in honour of the dead. Nithilan was too close to the situation and yet, should he stay away from preventing his death? Even if Mayan did escape the riot, he would still be dead over some time. Still, Nithilan didn't have the heart to let Mayan die. Nithilan himself was seated as if he were half-dead!

To the south of the burial ground, there appeared rings of golden white light waves. The landing platform of 'Veer Jadayu' started unfurling gradually.

Nithilan was seated with his laptop and he received an unexpected alarm notification from the Sirrius organisation's iris recognition centre. The notification flashed that some strange ingress had been observed. He probed deeper. He discovered that India's 120 crore people's iris data had been diverted to a third-party database, in Mumbai. He identified the mother computer responsible for this transfer using his microinvasive specialised software. The information startled him. Nithilan's fingers shook. The burial ground's silent dust formed a layer on his computer screen.

'Veer Jadayu' entered the burial ground chanting the Rig Vedic lines. Jaishankar stepped out cheerfully and shook hands with Govardhan. The boxes were loaded. Nisha Pilot and Govardhan got into their respective pockets.

'Nithi, come along,' Pramil invited.

'I am not coming.'

'Again? Are you in repeat mode? The train won't stop for long.'

Nithilan thought it over for a few seconds.

'I have an important assignment here.'

'Hey! You are talking as if you have come on an onsite assignment to the USA. Come along.'

'You go Pramil sir. Karthika madam will be waiting for you.'

Govardhan stuck his head out of the pocket and called Pramil. Not knowing what to do, Pramil shoved the 'Atharvana' that he was holding in his hands to Nithilan's lap and got into his pocket. Nithilan sat in that rock construction as a vestige of the future!

'Veer Jadayu' spread saffron light rays all around and got ready to launch. Just then a *valari* tore through the air from nowhere and attacked Govardhan who had stuck his head out of the window to watch the launch, slit Govardhan's throat, and beheaded him. The foxes seemed to be hiding in the forest for just this head; they came howling and dragged the head into the forest. Govardhan's headless body proceeded towards modern India.

Nithilan rose in panic from the rock building, put his laptop on the floor, and rushed to Jadayu. He knew he could not save the head from the foxes. He turned to observe the direction from which the *valari* came. Aanguthevan stood there straight with his sturdy shoulder muscles rippling. Pothum Ponnu, who stood right behind Aangu, faded into the forest like a vanishing ghost.

Nithilan picked the *valari* that had fallen into the thorny bushes and handed it over to Aanguthevan. Aangu wiped it clean of blood and tucked it back into his dhoti. It was a *valari* made of ivory. His father Aanachathan had retrieved the ivory *valari*, from the British government's Agrahara office and had gifted it to his children to play with.

38

5.00 a.m.

Mandayan, Karuvayan, and Kottavi helped the villagers hide the livestock—goats, cows, and hens—for protection. They sent the women and children to their relatives' houses in the neighbouring villages. Very few stayed back in the village. Vitti Vellaiya Thevar's people sharpened the weapons and buried them under the banyan tree in the Karuppu temple. Pothum Ponnu refused to go away from the Big House. Chinna Mayan stayed with Nithilan in the choultry.

6.00 a.m.

'What is this yellow insect, uncle?'

'Atharvana' was screaming continuously. Nithilan had spoken to Linga early that morning and had requested that he wanted to urgently speak to the prime minister. 'Your behaviour must suit your station,' chided Linga. The call got disconnected. In the next hour, he was invaded by calls. Nithilan ignored them. He was busy cooking biriyani and chilli chicken for Mayan.

'If I speak anything to that insect, it will convey the message to my people back home. It will also convey to me, what they have to say.'

'Is it a prattle-mouth insect?'

Chinna Mayan picked it up and inspected it. As the calls kept coming, a red light was blinking on its head. It was vibrating and shivering like a wet chicken. Mayan kept it back in its place in a flash.

Nithilan shut the doors and windows.

6.30 a.m.

Revenue officials came and sat on the common grounds.

The drummer who had been chased away by Kottavi,

continued from where he left.

'This is to inform all the villagers of Perumanallur, that you should come and register your fingerprints in front of the higher officials. Those who defy it will be handcuffed. This is a police order....'

His drum echoed across the village. They had placed a table and chair in the centre of the grounds and the register had been placed on it. There was an ink pad placed next to it for pressing the fingerprints and registering them. A bell was placed to indicate that the next person in line could step forward. Sindhupatti Inspector Nagamalai, Thirumangalam Sub-inspector Raja Desingu, and Usilampatti Sub-magistrate Venkatesan Anbu were seated in the chairs.

The elders and the young ones came to the grounds. They stared curiously at the register and the bell. 'If we refuse to place our fingerprints they might whack us on the head with the bell, Ding-dong!' was a comment from a young lad. The 'Ding-dong' sound spread like a forest fire and reverberated across the village. The village elders laughed out loud on hearing the sarcasm from the youth.

'Hey, constable! Have they come here as spectators for the popular *Valli's Wedding*, play? Demonstrate how to register their fingerprints.'

When Nagamalai shouted this instruction, Constable Mariappan opened the last page of the register.

'Hello villagers, make a note of this.'

He placed his thumb on the ink pad and placed the impression on the register. The children clapped their hands. Nagamalai was enraged.

'Bastards! Are we clowning around? Who is the village elder? Where are you lost? Ask everyone to line up.'

The village was silent. Nagamalai plonked himself back on

the chair. Mariappan was repeating the action of placing his thumb impression on the register robotically. 'Maybe I will be the lone person doing this until the end!' he cried internally. None stepped forward.

'You are going to consume all the ink. I am going to kill you for that.'

Nagamalai yelled at Mariappan. He wiped his hands and stood stiffly behind Nagamalai. Veerana Thevar and Cheeni Thevan approached the table.

7.15 a.m.

'Aiya, if someone is a criminal, please reveal his name. We will apprehend him ourselves and hand him over to you. If something has been stolen, give us the details. We will claim it back without charging you for the investigation. But we can't register our fingerprints.'

Special Judge Venkatesan wiped his glasses adjusted them and rose.

'As an elder of the village, kindly understand that this process and this Act is to ensure that no theft or criminal activities happen. This is a preventive measure. We have completed this all over India. Why is it that your village is asking so many questions and protesting?'

'When we had a famine, India didn't come to our aid. Kunjarathamma came and blessed us with gruel. Our people are our protection. Our people are well aware of our soil. They know the rains. But we don't know how to kneel and surrender to another. If you want to protect us, you are most welcome. Go ahead and secure and protect us. Suggest ways and means to save our goats and cows. Educate us to save our lands. Instead of doing any of these productive means, what are you going to do with our fingerprints?'

7.45 a.m.

The debate heated up. The armed forces came into the village with a lot of noise. Fifty cavalry and fifty rifle-carrying soldiers lined up. Vellaiya Thevar's people rushed to the banyan tree and retrieved the hidden spears and daggers.

Kaliyamman ridge was ready to be set ablaze.

'We are asking you one last time. Come and register your fingerprints and we can resolve this peacefully.'

Nagamalai raised his voice.

Mayandi Thevar's grandson, Muneeswaran, was fiddling around with the tail of a horse. The horse rider kicked the boy hard. He fell to the ground. Cheeni Thevan picked him up. The villagers were agitated. Mandayan used the sling in his catapult and aimed the stone at the bell placed on the table. The bell rolled to the ground with a gong. 'Hey stop,' pleaded Constable Mariappan. Nagamalai dragged Mandayan around and started beating him with his stick. Vellaiya Thevar's people attacked Nagamalai. Thirumangalam Sub-inspector Raja Desingu asked the cavalry force to charge. The horse riders tried to disperse the crowd. The horse hooves raised a sandstorm around. Karuvayan pushed Raja Desingu to the ground and the Sub-inspector screamed, 'Charge!' The first bullet was fired. It pierced Mayandi Thevar's abdomen and brought out his intestines. He held on to his intestines with one hand and ran to save Muneeswaran. The bullets started raining and corpses hit the ground. Virumayakkal was bringing water for the villagers and one of the soldiers kicked her out of the way. He stabbed her behind with the bayonet and shot her. She screamed 'Kanda!' and fell dead. Cheeni Thevan, who was hit by a bullet, was struggling for life. Mayandi Thevan carried him on his shoulder and ran into the forest to hide.

'Aiya, Mayandi! I will not survive this ordeal. You throw me in the drainage and save your life. Your intestines are sticking out. Undergo medical treatment and save your life.'

Cheeni Thevan insisted. Mayandi did not have the strength to carry him any further. Just as Cheeni Thevan had suggested, he laid him down under a neem tree near the drain. He held Cheeni's hands and gave him a farewell and Mayandi started running. On his way, he fainted.

It took a long time for the firing of the bullets to be silenced. The place was filled with smoke. The cavalry entered the village. They were joined by the police officers of Sindhupatti. The livestock were stolen. They also raided the houses and stole grains and women's ornaments.

The soldiers who entered the Big House tried to molest the women there. Pothum Ponnu fought with them tooth and nail and killed one of them with *aruvamanai* (the small sickle attached to a wooden plank used for cutting vegetables or meat). The lifeless man staggered down but his finger pressed the trigger and Pothum Ponnu was shot on the forehead. She fell with eyes wide open. The soldiers left from the Big House.

They approached the choultry where Nithilan was staying and tried to bang it open with their rifles.

'The person staying inside is Nithilan. He is a foreigner, who has come to practise silambam'.

Mariappan filled them in with this detail and so the soldiers banged the door once again in frustration and moved on to the next street.

8.45 a.m.

Thirteen corpses that were shot by bullets were arranged near the well under the portia tree. Five were grievously injured. All the dead bodies were loaded in one bullock cart and were sent to the mortuary in Usilampatti for post-mortem. The injured were admitted to a hospital.

About 200 villagers who had participated in the riot were seated under the banyan tree in the Karuppu temple in police custody. They were all tied together by one iron chain and were taken by foot to the Thirumanagalam police station.

9.00 a.m.

Nithilan opened the windows.

Bharat's Prime Minister, Home Minister, Home Secretary, Defence Minister, Sirrius head Mohan Janarthanan—all the political honchos had gathered in the tunnel workshop in Sanjay Van.

Nisha Pilot and Jaishankar stepped out of the train with Govardhan's body wrapped around by the Indian flag. They mourned his death by observing two minutes of silence.

Nisha Pilot briefed the prime minister about Govardhan's murder without sparing any details. The prime minister considered his death a national blemish. The prime minister ordered that a special task force be formed to go a 110 years back to the past to arrest Aanguthevan.

'Atharvana' continued to scream. When Linga accepted the call, Nithilan placed the request that he wanted to speak to the prime minister urgently. 'Act as per your station. You have no place in modern India. Die as a resident of Perumanallur.' Linga ordered so and disconnected.

The staff unloaded the 2,000 boxes. The task force officials inspected the boxes. Mohan Janarthanan invited the prime minister to place his thumb impression.

The prime minister raised his thumb to everyone around and went and placed it on the top of the first box.

'Wrong print! Please try again!'

This message was flashed on the box's screen.

'What is happening? The very first box seems to be spitting back at us!'

The staff started murmuring anxiously.

Mohan Janarthanan checked the box. The prime minister placed his thumb again.

'Wrong print! Access denied!'

The prime minister grinned wryly at Mohan and Linga. They were unsure about what to do next and pulled the second box around. That refused to open too! They tried opening ten boxes unsuccessfully.

Linga wanted to speak to Nithilan; it was critical and he tried reaching out to him desperately for nearly three hours. He held on to 'Atharvana' forcefully. Nithilan did not accept his call. The prime minister and the other ministers were waiting in the control room.

The bullock cart started moving towards the Usilampatti mortuary from Kaliyamman ridge. The thirteen corpses were stacked one next to another and one on top of another like rice sacks damaged in a cyclone or rain.

Cheeni Thevan's right hand was hanging out of the cart. Nithilan folded it and placed it on his body. Chinna Mayan was wailing 'My father!' and there was snot all over his nose and face. He walked slowly with Nithilan behind the cart. The running cart seemed like a gaping giant to him. He feared to walk along with it. Nithilan held his hands tightly. 'Atharvana' was constantly screaming. Nithilan pressed the button. Linga started talking agitatedly.

'What's happening, Nithilan?'

'Post-mortem is about to take place.'

'What?'

'I am explaining what is happening here…'

'I am not asking about that. None of the boxes are opening. What the hell is going on? What design is this? There is a big error in your programming. The prime minister and other ministers have gathered here. We have delegated an important responsibility to you. What are you doing there without attending the call?'

Nithilan placed 'Atharvana' in his pocket and helped them

unload the bodies by carrying them on his shoulder and taking them to the mortuary.

'Nithilan, are you there?'

'Yes! I am here! I am the only one here.'

When Nithilan placed Cheeni Thevan's body down, Chinna Mayan came around and hugged it and sobbed.

'The prime minister! I don't want to talk to anyone else other than him!'

Linga carried the 'Atharvana' into the control room. The prime minister agreed to speak with Nithilan.

'Nithilan, prime minister here. How are you?'

Nithilan moved to the neem tree that was diagonally opposite the mortuary. Chinna Mayan laid his head on his lap.

'Sir, as per the judgment of the Supreme Court, in the year 2017, the Right to Privacy was declared as a fundamental right.'

'Yes! I know.'

'It is the government's responsibility to protect that fundamental right. But I am sorry to say we have failed that fundamental duty towards the citizens!'

'What are you saying, Nithilan?'

'The Adayal data from the data warehouse of the Indian government, 120 crore people's iris data have all been sold to a social networking technology company called MeetaVerse!'

Sanjay Van stood still for a moment.

'How do I believe what you say, Mr. Nithilan?'

'The person who did this is none other than my boss, the owner of Sirrius, your home minister's dear friend, Mohan Janarthanan.'

The prime minister looked at Mohan, who was having tea. Mohan slowly kept the mug back on the table.

'Sir, Meeta and Mohan Janarthanan have joined hands to create a virtual city called MeetaBharat. They have peopled the city with the likes of our people. They reflect our talents and skills. They even have similar accomplishments. They are stealing India's identity and mirroring them and are building a virtual city. They want the people of the virtual city to have eyes, relatable to Indians, and Meeta had made that request to Mohan Janarthanan. He has agreed to sell all the iris data in our Adayal data centre to them. If you don't believe me, I have hacked the conversations that he had with Meeta. I have mailed it to your PMO ID. It isn't just that; if you happen to have a computer handy, ask him to log in. You take a close look at his city. Everyone in the city would be wearing dark shades. They have all been waiting to get iris and that's why they are without eyes and wear dark glasses. This is mentioned in paragraph 7 of their contract agreement. I have mailed that too. Mohan gets a share of the revenue generated from this imaginary city. To cut a long story short, Meeta has completely stolen Indian people's personal details, cultural and life practices, and India's multi-discipline secrets, and is aspiring to create a shadow nation, a virtual India. Mohan is an important partner in this venture.'

The prime minister wore virtual glasses and in Jadayu's workshop, he was looking at Mohan's virtual world on a computer. He saw infrastructure as described by Nithilan. He saw people sporting dark glasses. He went around the police station and hospital.

Nithilan explained every detail in clear and lucid English so that everyone at the workshop could understand:

'My fingerprint, my iris, my structure, thoughts, emotions, desires, and experiences have reached them as information and data. They don't need me as flesh and blood. They create a reflection of me in their world. Just as they throw away the dregs of the fruit after squeezing the juice, I lose value once my reflection is ready. My reflection starts functioning like me and a stage might come where I might have to follow the directions of my reflection. I may not be able to see what I choose with my own eyes; I might have to see only what my reflection's eyes dictate. My reality might be enslaved by the shadow that they have of me. I might be destroyed and tomorrow my reflection could become me. Their big data analysis has revealed that my reflection is more qualified to be their slave than I would ever be. That is their vision too. I have another suspicion too. I feel that the Jelly virus attack was created by Meeta (formerly known as FaceNool) institution. This is just my intuition. Their history is such. Some years ago, they started a plan called "Internet. All." They claimed that it would modernise the Internet. According to that they laid a condition that anyone who enters the Internet must enter with the permission of Meeta. When technical field experts and activists researched and pointed out that this "gateway" suggestion was an indirect means to get the whole of the Internet under Meeta's control, the plan was given up. But Meeta didn't stop with its efforts. They invested a huge capital in the undersea communication process. They signed huge spectrum contracts with every country. That was not sufficient. If one needed to take over a place, one had to first destroy it. They might have thought that, if they had to conquer the Internet, they had to disable the connections and equipment. Or the lost sheep amongst them could have planted this seed of poison in their minds. You must consider the fact that when the whole world was destroyed by the Jelly virus, Meeta-connections alone were functional. This is not my firm conclusion. The courts can hear this out. We may have plenty of differences amongst ourselves. My friend might want to form an Islamic nation. You may want to create a Hindu Rashtra. The Tamilians might create yet another Dravidian continent. We may set aside the religions and start afresh by naming nations based on the native tribes. The common people's revolution might choose right and wrong. But conquering the world wide web, stealing and ruling over personal data and thus dominating individuals and increasing multifold the hatred amongst us and making us their slaves and leaving us to dogs—all this is possible for Tech giants; corporations, and the higher officials who aid them together will become the common enemy of the present world. We need to realise this soon enough. We need to save the people from this shadow possession.

'I am observing the people here who are protesting against authority who want to capture their fingerprints. This protest shook my conscience. The purpose of their protest is different. Our people trusted us and without raising a question they surrendered their valuable personal data like fingerprints, iris and biometrics to the Indian government and so we need to be completely accountable to them. I fear this responsibility! My anxiety is that the data that we have gathered must be used only for productive means!'

'Nithilan, I wonder if you are seeing everything from a negative frame of mind.'

'No, sir! I am warning you that a great battle is about to ensue between people and their reflections. This is even more dangerous than the battle between man and machine.'

'What is the connection between this theory and opening the boxes?'

'Forgive me, Prime Minister! If you had placed your thumb and if the boxes had opened, you would not have heard me out, this far!'

'Then, are you the one who reprogrammed it?'

'Yes, sir.'

'What do you want?'

'They have set up a data centre in Mumbai and our iris recognition data are transferred from this centre to Meeta. Please bomb and destroy that centre immediately.'

The prime minister gave a stunned stare. He looked at the

home minister and Linga. Linga took over the 'Atharvana'.

'Nithilan, are we playing a video game here? How can we bomb a place on your say-so? We need to open the boxes immediately. Give us a solution for that.'

'I have mailed the Mumbai data centre address.'

The prime minister ordered the home minister to disable that centre.

'Nithilan, the prime minister will take due steps as per protocol. Please answer my questions first.'

'I haven't completed it yet. My second request—arrest Mohan Janarthanan and ensure that he cannot come out for a long time by giving him a life sentence. We should teach a definite lesson to those who want to enslave people using their data and the ones who are trading on it.'

The prime minister intervened.

'Nithilan, if whatever you have stated is the truth, we will take stringent actions against everyone involved, without any discrimination. That is my duty. You must stay with me and cooperate for that.'

Nithilan realised the moment's truth in the prime minister's words.

'If you want to open the boxes, I must come there. Send around 'Veer Jadayu.'

The call was disconnected.

The five injured villagers admitted to the Usilampatti hospital died despite medical attention.

The Mumbai data centre was completely neutralised and the staff working there were placed under arrest.

After the post-mortem, all eighteen bodies were buried in the same pit in the Pannapatti burial grounds.

An order was passed to keep Mohan Janarthanan under house arrest.

Nithilan lit earthen lamps around the cemetery stone of those who died in the riot. There should have been only sixteen lamps as per history. But thanks to Govardhan's murder two extra lamps were lit. Nithilan knelt to ask forgiveness by blaming himself for Govardhan's heinous crime. He sat on the mud, closed his eyes, and offered a grateful prayer.

'Eighteen questions opposing slavery are buried here.'

He used a firebrand and burnt this message on a wooden plank and stuck it to the mud.

Nithilan and Chinna Mayan travelled back to the choultry in the bullock cart that had carried the corpses.

00000000040

Just a few minutes before the Time Travel Train could depart the Usilampatti burial ground, with all the boxes loaded…

'Veer Jadayu' entered the burial ground chanting the Rig Veda lines. Jaishankar stepped down cheerfully and shook hands with Govardhan. The boxes were getting loaded. Nisha Pilot and Govardhan boarded their respective pockets.

'Nithi, come on, let's leave,' said Pramil.

'I am not coming.'

'Once again? What is with your yo-yo talk? The train won't stop for long. Come on.'

'I have an important work here.'

'Hey, don't blather as if you have come to the USA on an onsite assignment. Come along.'

'You leave, Pramil sir. Karthika madam will be awaiting you.'

Just a few seconds later Aanguthevan's *valari* beheaded Govardhan. Jadayu left.

Nithilan came directly to the Big House from the burial ground. He took permission to keep Chinna Mayan with him. All night he rewrote the programs that would open the container boxes.

'Nethili uncle, I am unable to sleep.'

Chinna Mayan came to him around midnight, rubbing his eyes.

'Come here.'

Nithilan sat him on his lap. Chinna Mayan went to sleep sucking his thumb. Nithilan tried to remove it from his mouth. But, Chinna Mayan immediately started sucking it again.

'What is this habit?'

'If I don't keep it in my mouth, the British would come and

forcibly take the fingerprint and register it, right? That's why I am sucking on it.'

Nithilan laughed at Chinna Mayan's fear.

'My nation's fate is in your thumb impression, Maya!'

'What are you saying, uncle?'

'You must come with me to my country.'

'Will I get jeerani in your place?'

'Why jeerani? You will get jangiri.'

'What is jangiri?'

'That is coloured jeerani.'

'Will you let me watch plays?'

'Sure!'

'Shall we take my father and mother along?'

'They won't come.'

'Mmhm…Ok!'

'Sleep well. Tomorrow morning, I will make briyani and chicken fry for you. After we finish lunch, we can leave for my place in the evening.'

'Will your train come?'

'It has to come.'

He went off to sleep. Nithilan started grinding the spices for the briyani by dawn. Nithilan had rewritten the programs such that, the boxes would open only with Chinna Mayan's thumb impression.

'Veer Jadayu' had brought Nithilan and Chinna Mayan safely back to Sanjay Van.

Two years later....

'I need an iced Milo.'

'I will have lemon tea.'

The waiter left after taking the orders from Senganthal and Nithilan.

'Why are you so restless? Next week is our wedding.'

'It's nothing.'

'Do not get onto the train and vanish again, because your people asked you to. Then I will have to tie the knot around my neck, myself.'

'Why are you in a sari?'

'I am practising to wear one properly.'

'You haven't draped it properly. But you look good.'

'Many thanks.'

The former principal secretary of the armed forces, Govardhan's second anniversary was being observed and it was televised on the café's TV screen.

'Nithi, you said that a special force was sent to seize Aanguthevan. What happened?'

'On the third day after the Perumanallur riot, Aanguthevan killed Inspector Nagamalai by stabbing him. The Madurai police arrested him. It was decreed that he would be punished in Penang's prison. When our Indian special force landed there, the ship had set sail from Tuticorin to Penang. Our folks had gone chasing them in another ship. Unexpectedly Aanguthevan escaped from everyone at the Penang harbour. They have information that he is in hiding in the Wallace Hills range. Both the current government and the past government of another timeline are searching him for the double murder charge.'

'Super! In case he moves to the future and commits a murder then he might be titled a tri-world criminal, one who has won time!'

'You will use this as a thumbnail and it would be convenient for you to do an episode on Aanguthevan, right?'

'I just happened to mention it. Just let it be. How is Chinna Mayan? Haven't seen him in a long while now.'

'He is doing good. Karthika has accepted him wholeheartedly but Pramil has his reservations.'

'You are his Nethili uncle! You, are there for him!'

'He has not settled down in school yet. I don't know what to do about that.'

'It was a mistake, that you brought him to the current times. On top of that, you have put him in a school. It is like encasing a river fish in an aquarium. Take a business class ticket in your 'Veer Jadayu' and leave him in his times, Nithi.'

'There is no one for him there, Senga.'

'We are the ones who have no relationship even with our folks who stay under the same roof. For them, the whole village would be one big family.'

Nithilan went quiet. Senganthal's iced Milo arrived. She scooped the dry Milo powder which came as a topping, with a spoon and licked it with relish.

'Are you a baby?'

'Yes. Ok, out with it. Why are you so dull? Did you not expect that we would come as far as a wedding? Your plan on ditching me midway didn't work, huh? Or is it the delayed arrival of the lemon tea?'

'You crazy girl! Mohan has been arrested for the past two years. But then even as lately as yesterday, some iris data from the

Adayal storage have been transferred to Meeta systems.'

'Isn't there a case against Meeta?'

'They have faced plenty of cases. They have come out of the Cambridge tangle!'

'Who supplies them the data?'

'I am unable to find that.'

'I read an article in *Now Times*, yesterday, Nithi. Some big social media organisations like Meeta have identified "Hero Agents" in every country and they are using these people for their cyber mafia activities. These Hero Agents are extraordinary geniuses in tech but smart thieves. They know every nook and cranny in cyberspace. The important information in this is…'

She sipped on her Milo.

'…the average age of these Hero Agents is anywhere between ten and thirteen!'

Nithilan's eyes widened.

'How come that age bracket, Senga?'

'In a situation where both parents are working, the kids are acquainted with cell phones and iPads by the time they are three or four years old. They step into the virtual world long before they get into schools. They enter that world when three, and by the time they are ten years old, they become veterans. Their brain development is amazing. Thanks to the gaming practices, they are well versed in guns, bombs, theft, murder, and dacoity. The brain development is devoid of human values. They resemble a mentally challenged person. Of course, they are mentally deranged. But the brain functions like a thirty-year-old adult seasoned in criminal activities. They have not been raised by their parents but by their imaginary characters. They are fake in the real world but true to their virtual world. None would suspect them because they are juveniles. Even if somebody did suspect them, they would sniff them out. They would magically vanish into hiding if need be.

They would pounce with the speed of light when it is time to attack. The good and bad that the world has never witnessed until now are going to emanate from them. They are dangerous kids!'

On their way back Hello FM was being played in the car, but Senga's Hero Agents were getting echoed in Nithilan's mind.

Movie director Rajamouli was giving an interview on the radio about his choice of actors for his movie *Mahabharata* and that was when Nithilan remembered Virumayakkal's story. In the story about Bheeman and Gadodgajan, Nithilan presumed that Gadodgajan who stole the goats was also a Hero Agent of sorts, as Senga informed. He smiled to himself at that thought. Nithilan's hunt to find the person stealing the iris data lies in Virumayakkal's story—the fact was yet to be realised by Nithilan himself!

Aagol II—*Machiavelli's story to be continued...*